THE PITFALL

Jon Forbes is a happily ma_ Hollywood when his cop fri_ about a gal named Mona h_ husband is in jail, and she k_ows _nat Mac is the cop who put him there. So Mac asks Forbes to set her up for him. Take her out, introduce her to him as a friend.

But that's where Forbes's troubles begin. Because happily married or not, Mona gets into his blood immediately. And he into hers. And now he's not only lying to his wife, but trying to avoid Mac as well. He and Mona have no idea where this will lead, but they both know it can't end well. But neither of them figure just how far Mac will go to get Forbes out of the way once he discovers his friend's betrayal. Nor what Forbes will do to protect his own.

"This is the most compelling, the most unusual, the most dramatic work of fiction I have read for years."
—*Denver Rocky Mountain News*

The Pitfall

JAY DRATLER

Introductions by
Jay Dratler, Jr. and
Timothy J. Lockhart

STARK
HOUSE

Stark House Press • Eureka California

THE PITFALL

Published by Stark House Press
1315 H Street
Eureka, CA 95501, USA
griffinskye3@sbcglobal.net
www.starkhousepress.com

THE PITFALL
Originally published by Thomas Y. Crowell Company, New York, and
copyright © 1947 by Jay Dratler. Reprinted 1949 in paperback by Bantam
Books, New York, and 1956 by Popular Library, New York. Copyright
renewed October 4, 1974 by Berenice T. Eunson (Berenice T. Dratler).

"The Author, Jay Dratler" © 2022 by Jay Dratler, Jr.
"Jay Dratler and *The Pitfall*" © 2022 by Timothy J. Lockhart

ISBN: 979-8-88601-008-4

Cover & Text design by Mark Shepard, shepgraphics.com
Proofreading by Bill Kelly

First Stark House Press Edition: November 2022

THE AUTHOR, JAY DRATLER

by Jay Dratler, Jr., his son

My father was a complex and sometimes a difficult man. He could be his own worst enemy. While working on the script for the movie *Laura*, he got into an argument with the imperious producer, Otto Preminger.

Both men were descended from German-speaking Jews. Both spoke German fluently. Preminger spoke English with an accent, my father with none.

The argument turned on a phrase in English—a difference over a single line. Exasperated by what he felt was improper interference in his writing, my father yelled at Preminger, "Don't tell me how to write English, you Kraut!"

Years later, he would tell that story with pride in his voice. It was not until I was in Harvard Law School that I understood what a failure of "people skills" my father had so proudly recounted.

That failure had consequences. Late in production, Preminger hired two other writers to "ghost" my father's nearly-completed script for *Laura*, thus diluting his screen credit. When the film got an Academy Award nomination for best adapted screenplay, my father was only one of three nominated. In any event, a "feel-good" musical with Bing Crosby, *Going My Way*, swept the Awards that year, including the one for best adapted screenplay.

My father never worked for Preminger or his studio again. To this day, you can read online notes of that era, recounting Preminger's view that my father couldn't write dialogue. But in fact his dialogue sparkled with brilliant and original gems, some of which he used in daily conversation with family and friends.

Whenever he wanted to damn something with faint praise, he would call it "better than a whop in the crotch with a mashie niblick" (a kind of golf club). When he wanted you to get off your duff and do something, he would exclaim, "Don't just sit there like a latke!" (A latke is a Jewish potato pancake, which sits rather heavily in the gut.)

I always thought that was a common Jewish expression until recently. Then my wife, who is far more immersed in American Jewish culture than I, informed me the expression was unique to my Dad. As she pointed out, it appears nowhere else in Jewish stories or literature.

You, the reader, can judge the quality of my Dad's dialogue for yourself. You'll find a lot of it, even in a novel like this one. My Dad was not addicted to long passages describing scenery or the internal rumination of his characters. He wrote according to the author's prime directive—"show, don't tell." That made his transition to screenwriting easy.

One thing not so apparent from my Dad's writing is his times. His United States was as different from today's as if it were on another continent.

He was part of a wave of first-generation Americans born of late-nineteenth-century Jewish immigrants from Central and Eastern Europe. We think he was born in 1911, but we don't know for sure. He fudged his birth date to make himself seem older than my Mom.

We do know that his own mother, Pauline, was born and raised in Vienna. She took my Dad back there every summer until he was fourteen. Hence his fluent and idiomatic German.

After he married my mother, the two visited Europe in the early thirties, just when Nazism was getting rolling in Germany and Austria. He was able to translate discreetly when strange German women called my mother a "whore" in German, apparently because she was wearing lipstick, rouge and bright-colored clothing.

Like most of the American Jewish writers, actors and producers of his generation, my father adored the United States. His family had grown up with stories of pogroms, ghettoes, legal exclusion, forced migration and various assaults upon ancestors. They were supremely grateful to be living in a free country, with freedom of religion and movement and (notwithstanding the occasional anti-Semitism) the ability to walk the streets of New York City unafraid.

So enamored were some show-business Jews of their new home, and so eager to fit in, that they changed their names to sound more "American." Bernie Schwartz became Tony Curtis.

My Father's time affected his life span, as well as his milieu. Most, if not all, of the miracles of modern medicine that we now take for granted came too late for him. Like many of his contemporaries, he smoked, he drank, and he ate a lot of meat and butter to enjoy his prosperity. He had his first heart attack at age 48 and died of his second, at 57, while visiting Puebla, Mexico. His ashes are entombed there in a roadside cemetery, in what was then a large village but is now a city of over half a million people. I hope to visit them before I, too, pass along.

My father's time was a far more innocent time than today, perhaps even a credulous one. The "black" in his "noir" genre came from within individuals' souls—their needs, their lusts, their pride, their temptations, their frustrations, and their dreams, however illicit or impossible. Their struggle was an internal one, and one among acquaintances, with a background of norms of behavior that everyone then took for granted.

So enjoy this journey back to a more innocent but no less human time. And if you can recall that time yourself, delight in it and mourn what we may since have lost, along with an innate sense of truth, the law and the right, all of which are under dispute.

—August 2022
Santa Fe, New Mexico

JAY DRATLER AND THE PITFALL
By Timothy J. Lockhart

For fans of crime stories there is a special delight in watching a film noir from the genre's original golden age, the mid-1940s through the 1950s. But often those films produce a double pleasure by leading the viewer to discover excellent novels and short stories that were the movies' source material. Thus, *Out of the Past* (1947) can lead you to Geoffrey Homes's 1946 novel *Build My Gallows High*. Or *The Killers* (1946) can lead you to Ernest Hemingway's 1927 short story with the same title. This is how I discovered Jay Dratler's fine noir novel *The Pitfall* (1947): by watching the fine noir film *Pitfall* (1948).

The Pitfall is a tense psychological thriller featuring successful Hollywood screenwriter Jonathan "Jon" Forbes. His friend "Mac" MacDonald, a Beverly Hills police officer who occasionally gives Forbes crime material for his screenplays, tells him about a beautiful woman, Mona Smiley. MacDonald wants to make a play for her while her husband, Bill, is in jail for purse-snatching, but MacDonald is the one who arrested him, and Mona has seen her husband in his custody at the jail. MacDonald doubts that he will be able to seduce Mona unless Forbes has seduced her first—"knocked her over," as the cop puts it to Forbes in his heavy-handed way.

Forbes, a happily married man with a three-year-old daughter and another child on the way, is reluctant, initially refusing MacDonald's suggestion. But the cop's descriptions of Mona are so enticing that eventually Forbes agrees to call her. He invites her to a bar, and when he spots her there, he likes what he sees: "How can I tell you what the first sight of her did to me? Is there such a thing as a depraved virgin? Because she looked depraved and she looked virginal. And I only saw her from the neck up. It was in her eyes and in her lips, and in the taut way she held her head. Eyes gray and fathomless; and hair blacker than the polished belt Mac wore."

Bound by convention, however, Forbes is too scared to go through with actually meeting Mona. But the next day he screws up his courage, calls her again, and arranges another meeting. And so, despite the scruples they each confess to the other, they begin a torrid affair.

Forbes often thinks of Mona as a "tigress," and, as a college-educated man, recalls lines from William Blake's poem *The Tyger* when he does. (He also name-checks Auguste Rodin, Sergei Rachmaninoff, and the lesser-known José Iturbi.) To spend time with Mona, Forbes lies to his wife, to his co-workers, and, most ominously, to MacDonald, who thinks he and Forbes have a deal.

But Forbes, smitten, wants her all to himself. And, as any fan of noir fiction or film could guess, things go badly from there, vividly illustrating the central tenet of noir: that fundamentally good people ensnare themselves by knowingly doing wrong.

The movie *Pitfall*, stylishly directed by Andre de Toth—who also made *House of Wax* (1953), one of the earliest and most successful 3D films—follows the general outline of the novel but makes a few changes, most for the better. In the film, John (not Jon) Forbes, well played by Dick Powell, is an insurance adjuster bored with his life and perhaps even his wife, Sue. In the novel she has been bedridden for four months as she deals with a difficult pregnancy. In the movie, however, Sue, played effectively by Jane Wyatt, is an active wife and mother who tries to tease her husband out of his boredom. Early in the film she lightly responds to his spur-of-the-moment suggestion that they run off to South America, saying, "Not today." In the movie their young daughter Ann is replaced by a somewhat older boy named Tommy, but in both cases Forbes has a close relationship with his child, so close that Mona comments on it in the novel.

In the film, Forbes meets Mona Stevens, engaged to Bill Smiley, an embezzler, after MacDonald, a cop turned PI, learns that Smiley used the stolen money to buy expensive things for his bride-to-be: a fur coat, dresses, an engagement ring. Oh, and there's also a motorboat named *Tempest* that Mona has lovingly repainted and on which she takes Forbes for a wild ride the day they meet. The boat outing, for which he wears a business suit and hat, seems to symbolize the out-of-the-ordinary experiences he craves.

Lizabeth Scott, called in one of her obituaries "the most beautiful face of film noir during the 1940s and 1950s," plays Mona to perfection as a smart, sensitive woman who is also strong and brave. The affair that the movie Mona has with Forbes is less steamy than in the novel, where Mona is depicted nude more than once. But in both there is no mistaking the intensity of their passion even though the two realize that the heat will eventually burn them.

In the role of MacDonald, Raymond Burr magnificently captures the oily evil of the competent but crooked PI, who comes across as a fat spider waiting patiently for Mona to fly into his web. She wants nothing to do with him, but that does not stop him from pursuing her and using Forbes and Smiley as pawns in his deadly game.

Jay J. Dratler was born in New York City on September 14, 1911 (some sources give 1910), to a mother who was Austrian by birth. He attended the University of North Carolina at Chapel Hill; later he studied at the Sorbonne and the University of Vienna, and from those experiences he gained fluency in French and German.

According to a brief biography by Bruce Eder at fandango.com, Dratler "took up residence in Vienna in the '30s and was very much a part of the café society that existed there before the German invasion of Austria" in 1938. His son, Jay Dratler, Jr., has related how his father, as a young man, "smuggled out a large amount of currency for a good friend by hiding the money inside a rubber bag suspended in a toilet tank on a moving train."

Upon his return to the United States, Dratler worked as an editor for a New York publisher, translated two nonfiction books from German into English, and published his first two novels. At the beginning of the 1940s he moved to Hollywood, where he became a successful novelist and screenwriter. He published seven novels (*The Pitfall* being his third), wrote numerous screenplays, and turned out more than twenty TV scripts. Dratler won an Academy Award and an Edgar Allan Poe Award for his screenplay of the 1948 movie *Call Northside 777* and received an

Oscar nomination for his screenplay of the 1944 movie *Laura*—both good examples of classic film noir.

Toward the end of his life, Dratler, who had added Spanish to his list of languages, moved to Mexico. He died of a heart attack in Mexico City on September 25, 1968, at the relatively young age of 57, leaving his widow, Berenice, and their daughter and son. His body was returned to New York.

Dratler's novel *The Pitfall* is superbly written with well-rounded characters, a tightly ticking plot, sharp sentences and crisp paragraphs. Although many books—too many—are described as being hard to put down, *The Pitfall* truly is.

The reader is enthralled, seeing what Jon Forbes does not. As he obsesses about Mona, his tigress, and as they both fall deeper and deeper into the dark and deadly trap they make for themselves, Forbes does not reflect on the age-old practice of tiger hunting. But surely he is aware, as an educated, cultured, and undoubtedly widely read man, that one well-known way of hunting tigers is with a pitfall.

—August 2022

Note: *For Bruce Eder's biographical note on Jay Dratler, see www.fandango.com / people / jay-dratler-181046 / biography.*

Timothy J. Lockhart is a lawyer and former U.S. Navy officer who worked with the CIA, DIA, and Office of Naval Intelligence. Author of the novels *Smith* (2017), *Pirates* (2019), *A Certain Man's Daughter* (2021), *Unlucky Money* (2022), and *Evil Intentions Come* (scheduled for 2023), all from Stark House Press, he lives in Norfolk, Virginia, with his wife and daughter.

The Pitfall

JAY DRATLER

CHAPTER 1

I'm not the kind to remember dates, but never forget last February sixteenth. Because a man has about twenty-thousand days to live, and on that Friday, somewhere in the back of my head, I heard the snip of a giant scissors, and I knew there weren't many days left for me anymore. Or maybe it only seemed that way afterward.

What happened that day? Nothing much. The planets whirled on in their orbits. Sunspot activity was normal. The earthquake fault under Los Angeles didn't move a quarter of an inch.

But the phone rang. And that started the whole chain of events that wrecked me.

On that February sixteenth I had a good job writing scripts for Twentieth-Century Fox; I had a wonderful blonde wife and a little blonde girl, not yet four; I had money in the bank, owned my own house; and I had a future. I don't want to make it sound as if we were the family of Whistler's Mother—but we had something. And I still can't understand how a phone call could have destroyed it all.

I know what happened—but I don't know why or how. All I can give you is my side of it. I'm not even sure I remember all of it clearly because, right up to the end, I never knew it would be that important. I never even knew what hit me.

The day it started, I had just finished dictating a couple of pages of script to Kate, my secretary, at home. It wasn't good writing, but it was adequate—because I knew I would stay up all that night to do it over again. I do my best work at night, when it's quiet and there's nothing on the radio that I want to hear, and when I can't find any excuses for not working. I've been doing it for years. I generally go to sleep in the early morning and put a sleep mask over my eyes to keep the light out, and some wax-and-cotton ear stopples into my ears to keep the noise out. Sure, it's neurotic. What writer isn't?

Anyway, it was about three o'clock in the afternoon when the phone rang. Kate answered it, and then turned to me, holding her hand over the mouthpiece. "Do you want to talk to a Mr. MacDonald?"

For a minute I didn't recognize the name. Then I remembered he was a detective I had met through Fred Swift, a writer friend of mine. A couple of months after that I heard he had joined the Beverly Hills police force. Then I began to see him riding around in the white-sided police car, and now and again I'd stop and talk a while with him.

I picked up the phone. "Hello, Mac."

"Hello, Jon." His voice was heavy and pleasant. "Can you talk?"

That surprised me a bit. "Sure, why not?"

"Remember what we talked about a few weeks ago?"

I remembered a lot of things, but I didn't know what he meant.

"The girl in the bungalow," Mac said.

He had told me about a lonely girl who had been unable to make her way in pictures. Broke and despondent, she had tried to commit suicide. Mac got there in his police car in time to save her. He wrote it up as an accident, for favors rendered.

I was still puzzled, but I told him I remembered.

"Are you busy this afternoon?" he said.

For a second I couldn't answer. I was pretty sure there was a tie-up between the question and the girl in the bungalow. "No," I said, "not very."

"How about coming down and meeting me and we'll gab a while?"

"Sure," I said. "When?"

"Four-thirty be all right?"

"Fine," I said. "Where?"

"Doheny and Wilshire. You can park over near the Horace Heidt place. I'll pick you up there."

"Right. See you later.

I hung up.

That was it; as simple as that. What was wrong with it? As a writer, I was interested in Mac; he had stories to tell. About crime, and whores, and prominent picture people who got into jams. I liked to sit in his police car, parked on Wilshire Boulevard, with passersby staring at me as if I were a fresh-caught Dillinger, or at the very least a Peeping Tom. I noticed that most of the women who saw me usually took a second look—not at me, but just at a man who seemed to be under arrest. It interested them.

And Mac had some, really good yarns to tell. He was the one who told me about Tripler, one of the major studio producers. This was a couple of years ago, when L.A. was really rotten. Tripler was out with another woman one night, when he had told his wife he was working at the studio. Driving to a hotel, slightly crocked, he ran into another car. So he called some people to pull him out of it. It took no time at all to fix it. The car was hauled away and a bunch of mechanics worked all night fixing it. The girl was taken home in a cab. But Tripler was badly bruised in the face. What was he going to tell his wife?

They fixed that, too. They sent out a couple of plainclothes dicks, who stood on a corner of Main Street waiting for a likely sucker. A Mexican came along, and they jumped him. They beat the hell out of him, tossed him in the can, and booked him for assaulting Tripler. Mrs. Tripler and the rest of movie town were highly indignant; it was getting so a man wasn't safe on the streets anymore. The Mexican got three months.

Mac had lots of yams like that—like the one about the girl in the bungalow, too.

I kept thinking about that. What did he want? Did he think I was interested in that bungalow girl? Because I wasn't. I'd been around, but not lately. My life was set. Complete. Happy.

And I wasn't ashamed of it. A lot of people are. They think it's dull and corny to settle down. Maybe it was because they didn't have what I had.

Part of what I had came running up the stairs shortly after Mac phoned—thirty-four pounds of blonde, pig-tailed girl with a solemn determination to get to be four-years-old very quickly.

You'd be surprised at the things that can be done with a child that young. Most men are away at work all day, and they never find out. A writer stays home a lot, and he can give his child more time. A child's mind is like a sponge, hungry to learn, to know, to understand; they shouldn't be held back. They shouldn't be forced, either. I just played games with Ann—making a peek-a-boo game out of reading and writing. I'd tell her to hide and not to peek until I finished writing out a word in big block letters. And she'd be fascinated, trying to peek, trying to see the letters and read them. By this time she could read and write about thirty words.

That's something to have—pride and warmth and love—the kind of love most of us wish we'd had when we were kids. Love that is understanding.

All right, I'm the father again—running off with kid stories. But that was part of what I had.

The other part was Sue, my wife. Even now, five months pregnant, she was slim and delicate and small. But somehow, after a time, the appearance of someone you love is a triviality. She's just beautiful, and you let it go at that. It's the other things that count—being able to talk, to tell her everything that's in your heart—everything.

We're most of us lonely, never able to communicate—locked up in our heads and in our tongues. We're so many people at once, every one of us. We're what we really are; and then sometimes we act and talk as we'd like to be; and then again we act and talk as other people think we are.

With her, I was me—always. No holding back; no lies; no slipping apart in time.

All right, maybe I can't explain it. But it was there; and it was something I treasured. We didn't have one of those half-and-half marriages.

That's a fine buildup. That's a fine treasure. What kind of a thing can a man treasure that can be wrecked by a phone call?

When I started out to keep the date with Mac, it was raining. By the time I turned into Wilshire, the sun was out feebly, the way it was on many days in winter—as if somebody had lit a large match in Santa Monica. But it was out, anyway.

The streets were crowded in Beverly—especially at Saks Fifth Avenue. The afternoon crowd of wives poured across Wilshire, or jockeyed their big cars around as if they were lethal weapons.

I was right on time when I passed the stop light at Doheny and Wilshire. Cars were parked on all corners, so I went past the Horace Heidt place and found a spot in front of a little dry-cleaning store. I shut off the motor and waited.

After a while, I turned the radio on, and right off again. I was bothered and a little excited about this meeting. It sounded like police business or hanky-panky of some kind. With Mac, it could be anything.

He wasn't just an ordinary cop. When I met him at Fred's house, he proved that. He was a college graduate, and there were a lot of other things he could have taken up. Engineering, for one thing. But he was interested in criminology, and he became a private dick. He liked it. He liked nothing else. You could tell that from the way he discussed his work; and he was well-grounded in it, too—Lombroso wasn't someone he'd heard of; he knew Lombroso, and understood him.

Yet, somehow, Mac wasn't the type for it. He was a heavy-set man of about forty; who wore good clothes and fine shoes. He was self-possessed, and good humored, but when he laughed he made it sound like a recently acquired characteristic. He was more inquisitive than anyone I'd ever met—but in a detached and inoffensive manner. Impersonal. I remember he asked me question after question about my background. Later, Fred said he did that with everyone he met—card-indexing them in his mind, with all the details, for future reference. Just in case. I had a feeling that he might trap you with a lie-detector on a simple statement about the weather.

After a while, when I looked up, the police car was alongside me, double parked, and Mac was looking at me. I don't know how long he'd been there. People on the sidewalk gawked.

"Follow me around the corner," he said.

He drove off slowly, waiting while I started and curved out. Then I followed him around into the next block. He pulled up between two driveways, leaving me enough room to get in behind him.

I turned my motor off and then got into the police car with him. We shook hands.

"How are you, Jon?"

"Fine. What's new?"

He shrugged. "Nothing much. Seen Fred lately?"

"Few days ago. He's working at Universal."

I watched him curiously. He had lots of muscle on him; he was big. His face looked taut and hard, without a wrinkle in it anywhere. Like a football bladder filled with sand, and just as expressionless.

"He's a talented guy, that Fred," Mac said. "Good writer."

I nodded. "He knows his stuff."

Over the radio a metal clip held a sheaf of papers listing the numbers of stolen cars. To the left there was a copy of the daily police bulletin. This one had the picture of a bitter, gaunt man of about fifty. George Moreno. Wanted for armed robbery.

We gabbed a while—about why I hadn't seen him these past few weeks. He'd been transferred to this Doheny district. Then he talked about the young kids who were making police work dangerous—hopped-up kids with guns. The average age of criminals in L.A. had dropped from twenty-eight to eighteen. An ex-con will throw his gun away the minute the cops approach, because he knows possession of firearms adds years to his sentence. But a punk kid will shoot to kill; he's under age anyway, a juvenile, and can get away with almost anything.

The radio squawked. "Car 13. Code 1. Car 13. Code 1."

"What's that mean?" I said.

"Call your station," he said.

Mac went on. About Beverly Hills having to put on six more police cars lately; crime had increased five-fold.

But he was talking as if making up his mind about something. Waiting for an opening. He was completely relaxed. His uniform was immaculate. The cap was set straight on his head. And even after he had been sitting behind the wheel for hours, there wasn't a wrinkle in his trousers. The wide black belt with its triple row of holes for the three prongs of the buckle was polished to a high glow. The holster and revolver hung behind him.

After a long pause, he looked at his watch. "Getting late."

I didn't offer any help.

"Got something that might interest you," he said finally. "Happened about a month ago."

I leaned back, listening.

The story he told me didn't make much sense. There had been two purse snatchings in Beverly Hills. Amateur jobs, because the two men would run out of an alley toward the victim, and one would shout, "This is a stick-up!" Then he'd grab the purse and beat it. Mac said purse snatchers never yelled "stick-up" if they knew their business. They just grabbed and ran.

Anyway, about a month ago the cashier of a local restaurant was walking down Rodeo Drive late at night. Two men jumped out of an alley; one yelled, "This is a stick-up"; and they got her purse.

But she got to a phone at the Brown Derby, and the patrol cars surrounded the area. "We caught the two men on the next block—two men about thirty years old, well-dressed and nice looking. Amateurs. Named Garner and Smiley."

"What happened to them?" I asked.

"We didn't have anything on them. No previous record. So the judge gave it to them easy. Six months—with three suspended."

"Did you get the woman's money back?"

He nodded. "Sure. But we never worry about that; we just want the guy who took it."

He paused now, looking out of the window. I just waited. Was this what he wanted to tell me?

He kept looking out of the window. People who lived on the block were stopping to stare at the car and then moving off again reluctantly. A police car was an outrage perpetrated on their respectability. And they were curious.

So was I.

"Come on, Mac," I said. "What's on your mind?"

He turned in the seat, facing me more. Then he said he had a broken schedule now—five days in the car, and one day, Saturday, on the jail detail. So he saw the purse snatchers—Garner and Smiley. They were not confirmed criminals, and they were pretty certain to keep straight in the future—so they were made trusties, on the kitchen force.

"A couple of weeks ago, Smiley's wife came up to see him." He stopped and the tip of his tongue raced around the curve of his lips. "She's one of the most beautiful girls I've ever laid eyes on." Now he looked away from me again, off in the distance, but I couldn't see his eyes, just the turn of his head.

He went on. "Built like a jig, long and lean."

"What's a jig?"

"A nigger girl. Long and slim—and she walks like an animal."

I grinned at him. "We're waxing poetic, Mac."

He just shook his head. Then he leaned over, picked up the microphone from the hook on the dashboard, and pressed the button. The generator in the back of the car whirred.

"Car 28 out of service," he spoke into the mike.

He waited until the answer came. "Car 28 okay."

"What's that mean?" I asked.

"If they have any calls for me, they'll give them to some other car in the neighborhood. Until I call back in. If I'm spotted on this side street, I'm out of service. No trouble." He hung up the mike.

His voice got faraway again. "Yeah … She's fresh and young, about twenty-three … built out of bricks. Full lips. She's about five feet, three and a half. Black hair. Wears clothes, too."

"That's damned white of her," I said. "Otherwise, she'd *really* be driving you crazy."

"You know what I mean. Not flash; not chippie."

I nodded. Something had happened to Mac. Despite his education, no man can do that kind of work without getting a wide streak of cop. For instance, women were all chippies or tails or hustlers or maybe worse. He had developed that kind of outlook.

Now that I think about it, he developed other kinds of cop attitudes, too. I remember once he told me about another cop, a friend of his, he said. This friend was transferred downtown to another police car, with the regular driver. First day out, the driver laid it on the line. "How you fixed for dough?"

"Fine," Mac's friend said.

"Can you use some more?"

"Who can't?"

The driver then turned the car up a side street and just pulled up and parked, without saying anything. Mac's friend sat there a while and then wanted to move on.

"In a while," the driver said.

After about a half hour, a woman came out of a Spanish house they were parked in front of. She walked up to the police car and dropped an envelope into the back seat. Then she went right in again.

The driver started off, telling Mac's friend to pick up the envelope. There were two tens in it.

"One for you and one for me," the driver said.

"What for?"

"That was a whorehouse we were parked in front of. As long as the police car stays there, no customers will go into the house. The lieutenant gets his share, we get to get ours."

That was the story Mac told about his friend. But even when he first told it, I wondered whether there was any friend.

Anyway, cop or no cop, Mac had been hit. He was more than interested in that dame. He was hooked. I didn't even have to start him talking again. He poured.

"After she left the jail that day, I talked to Garner, the other guy. Just casually.

"'Nice wife your partner has,' I said.

"'Yeah. Pretty. But it's tough on Smiley,' he said.

"So I asked him 'Why—does she play around?'

"He said no, but she was hot as a firecracker, and her husband was worried about what she'd do while he was in jail—whether she'd find somebody else to take it out on."

He looked at me to see my reaction. He got none. He went on anyway.

"When she came into the jail last Saturday, she leaned over my desk while I wrote out the visitor's permit. She asked for a cigarette. I said I didn't have any, but I got one for her." He paused again, and took a deep breath. "You know what she said? Get this. She took a drag, and then she said, 'First cigarette I've had in three days. I nearly went crazy.' And I said, 'From not smoking?' And she started walking away. 'That's part of it,' she said."

It didn't seem particularly startling to me. She might have said it innocently; probably she did.

I shrugged. "Why don't you find out," I said. "If you're interested in her."

"I can't," he said. "But that's the setup. She's alone in town, doesn't know anybody. They just came from the East. Her husband's in for another six or eight weeks. She's lonely, and just waiting for somebody to light a match to her."

"Well, light it," I said impatiently.

"Me?" He looked surprised. "I can't. They don't go for cops, you know that. They're scared. Anyway, if I went plainclothes, she'd still recognize me. She's seen me at the jail."

"That's tough, Mac," I said.

"Maybe. But I was thinking that somebody else could get to her, knock her over, and then I could move in."

Oh, I didn't hold my breath or faint. But for a few minutes I couldn't have told anybody what time it was. Here the guy was hooked—and he couldn't get to her. But he was perfectly willing to let someone else get to her, so he could get to her next. It didn't add.

I pulled a pipe out of my pocket and chewed on the stem. "Meaning me, Mac?"

He looked out the window. "How's your wife?"

"Fine," I said, without thinking. Then I thought, all right, I thought plenty. Sue almost had a miscarriage; she was still taking those Pranone tablets, and opium. She'd been in bed for over three months, not allowed to move at all.

"I get the connection."

He nodded. "I thought you'd be interested."

I'd talked to the guy quite a bit; I know he deals with tough people and he's not too sensitive; but this knocked me off balance.

"You could meet her," he said, "get to her, and then some night I'd happen to meet you when you're out with her. And you introduce me. I take it from there."

I wasn't going to duck it anymore. "Look, Mac, you know damned well you could do it yourself. You don't need me. What's on your mind?"

"Okay. Okay. She knows me. I caught Smiley. If I get messed with her, she'd have me by the short hairs. Ripe for a shakedown. But if you knocked her over first, I could move in and be in the clear. We could both have some fun."

Well, there it was. Straight. I wonder how many people, making a little slip like that, fall into the hands of cops like this one. Or worse than this one. Because Mac had a background, a decent upbringing, and he'd never been short of money. Ignorant cops might have another excuse; but Mac was educated, and in certain ways he was damned clever. Too damned clever.

"If you got a look at her," he said then, "you wouldn't even be thinking about it."

I shook my head. "Yes, I would. I'd be thinking about me." I put the pipe away and lit a cigarette. "And this isn't for me, Mac." That was a good way to say it; not that I was morally superior to him, but that the circumstances didn't suit me.

"Why not? Scared?"

"You named it. I am. I'm not that adventurous. Any man who loves his wife so much he'll go out and snatch purses for her—especially a man who isn't a criminal—well, he loves her a lot, Mac. And he'll very likely kill any son-of-a-bitch who moves in on him."

"Oh, that's crap. Purse snatching is a punk's racket. Nobody with guts ever does it. Robbing old ladies? Why, they'd rather take their chances on a longer rap. This kid's yellow. He wouldn't hurt anybody."

"Maybe.... But I still say it's not for me."

Mac looked away. "She's a nice dish. Leaves a good taste in your mouth."

The way he said it, he seemed to be tasting her. He licked his lips afterward.

We sat quietly for a few minutes. Then he leaned over and picked up the mike again. The generator in the back of the car sounded much louder now. "Car 28. In," he said.

The metallic voice came back from the central office. "Okay. Car 28 back in service."

He hung up the mike.

After that, we stayed away from the topic. But he was restless now, and a little bit annoyed. He kept looking at his watch all the time. So I took the hint and told him I had to go.

We shook hands.

"I'll see you, Mac," I said.

"Sure."

He drove off, and I got back into my car. But I sat there for a while, thinking how close I'd come to getting into something dangerous. I was horrified at the possibilities.

He gave me a look into a world that was like a cesspool or maybe a jungle, where a soft guy like me would get his guts ripped out. When I was younger I might have been excited by something like this, and I might not have been too scrupulous. I don't think I would even have thought twice about it. I'm not sure. I was a little older now; a little more cautious, and I had a lot more to protect. I had people I didn't want to hurt; people who were my own. And it had taken most of my thirty-five years to learn I never wanted to hurt anyone else.

Still, I shouldn't have been so shocked. Things like that went on every day. It's just that it was a long time since one of them had come up and hit me in the teeth.

I drove home to safety.

My house was safety; my family was safety. Everything about the way I lived was safe. When I came through the front door, everything was right. Even the disorganization of my desk was a pattern; a normal pattern. Order.

But that meeting with Mac had knocked me out of my routine. I couldn't do any work on the script. I kept thinking about the Smileys. That was real; not a movie script. That woman was real, and so was her husband, slinging slops as a trusty in the Beverly Hills jail.

It wasn't pretty—with a studio orchestra caressing your heartstrings on the sound track. Adrian didn't do the costumes. The Hays office hadn't yet gotten at the script. And somehow I knew Mac was going to get to that woman, and I felt sorry for her.

The whole thing was so out of my world, I couldn't get my mind off it. At twelve that night, I was still goosing the typewriter keys, changing a line here and there, without making any improvements. And I was behind in my work already. I didn't like that. I didn't like disappointing Brawley, my producer, who was one of the decent executives in the picture business. But, still, I didn't want to turn in anything I didn't like. It wasn't only that I like to feel a studio is getting its money's worth; but I like to do my best because I want to be able to look into a mirror without feeling ashamed.

So I stayed at the typewriter. Two o'clock. Three o'clock. Four o'clock.

But I didn't work.

I was trying to figure how as callous a man as Mac could go down the line that far for a woman. I figured she must be quite a piece of woman.

Then I started wondering about her, making her more beautiful in my mind, more desirable than any woman could be. She had to be that way. I kept comparing her to a lot of women I'd known and seen around. I was just tense enough and hungry enough to keep wondering. A sweet girl, a helpless kid with another helpless kid for a husband. How helpless was he? How adequate for her? By now, I had him pegged as a punk kid, and he was shrinking in size every time I thought of him. Not half a man. Unable to support her. Snatching a purse. Putting her in such a position, bait for a cop like Mac.

When I went up to bed, the daylight was knifing through the openings in the drawn curtains. Sue had put my glass of milk on my night table; the sleep mask and ear stopples were laid out. That's the kind of attention I got when I was working.

I got into bed, listening to her breathing regularly in the other twin bed. And pretty soon it was the Smiley woman breathing—heavily, fretfully, tossing around, wanting him back, or wanting someone else.

I was a long time falling asleep.

CHAPTER 2

It was after eleven when I got up the next day. Kate was waiting in the den with the pages I had dictated the day before. I asked her whether Mac had phoned. She said no.

I had my breakfast and then took the script out into the patio. The sun was hot, the sky clear. The trees were polka-dotted with the light-green tips of leaves coming out.

I went inside again and asked whether Mac had phoned. Kate said no.

While I was in the shower, I suddenly began to wonder why I was expecting a call from Mac. I couldn't figure it. But when I went downstairs, I asked her again. It was still no.

Way back when I was a kid, I read a story about a great surgeon who was performing a trepanning operation in a tent on a battlefield. He had the top of the patient's head off when a centipede dropped off the roof of the tent and landed right on the exposed gray matter. He was going to take it off with a tweezer, but his young assistant stopped him. He pointed out that the minute the tweezer touched the centipede, it would writhe and struggle, and its little claws would sink into the soft gray tissue and rip it up. The surgeon agreed, but what else was there to do? Picking up a leaf, the assistant held it steadily over the exposed brain. Slowly, the centipede crawled onto it, without damaging the tissue.

Well, there I was with this thing like a centipede in my brain. Mac had put it there. I had no leaf. And every time I tried to get the thing out, it writhed and jabbed its claws in deeper.

If I could have gotten to work, concentrated on it, that would have taken the place of the leaf. But I couldn't. Going to the studio didn't help either. The office was waiting for me, the typewriter smiled at me with its round black and white teeth, and I kept picking up the trade papers, magazines, newspapers, and anything else that would distract me. It was Saturday and there wasn't another writer on the Fox lot. But Brawley, my producer, was there.

After a while, I went over to Brawley's office. He's a thin, ascetic-looking guy who doesn't think enough of himself; which should fit him for canonization in this town. He's got a good story mind; he knows film cutting, direction, and production; and he's a gentleman. But he's quiet and modest and the Hollywood crowd doesn't get him. He lives a normal family life, and he has yet to lay his first stock girl, and he respects writers. With a guy like that, you have to level.

Telling him I hadn't worked was easy. Telling him why was another story. I didn't even try. I just told him I was having trouble and felt guilty about it. Looking me over carefully, he shrugged. He told me not to get hysterical about it; relax. I was pushing too hard. Sure, he was disappointed; he wanted the script. But he'd rather have it good; and he knew he'd get it soon and it would be good.

For that kind of producer, a writer knocks his brains out.

At least, I tried to.

But when I got back to the office, I again automatically asked Kate, who had come over with me.

"Anybody call?"

"No, he didn't," Kate said.

For some reason, it griped me. "Who didn't?"

"MacDonald," she said.

"Damn you, mind your own business!" I stomped into my inner office.

Her voice came after me. "Yes, sir." Very softly.

That stopped me. I always told her to call me by my first name when we were alone; never "Mr." unless others were present—because they might misunderstand. The "sir" was a backhand across the face.

"Sorry," I said.

She didn't answer. But it was the first time we'd ever had anything like that happen. I liked that girl; she was intelligent and helpful and thoughtful.

What the hell was the matter with me?

Brawley's confidence braced me, and I wasn't worried about the script anymore. I knew I'd lick the story. I've never met one that couldn't be pounded into shape if you beat your head against it long enough and if you made real people live in it.

So I felt relieved—and able to give my entire attention to Mac. That's what happened, anyway. I went to bed early, and spent my time just lying there, without my sleep shade on, staring up at the ceiling.

Sue turned toward me. "Jon."

"Hmmmmm?"

"What's the matter?"

"Nothing, dear."

"I just happened to wake up and I could tell by your breathing that you weren't asleep."

"Can't sleep."

"Having trouble?"

"Not much. Brawley was swell about it."

"Then stop thinking about it. Get a good night's rest and start fresh tomorrow."

"I'll try."

There was a pause.

"Want anything?"

I snickered. "Ummmm-hmmmmmmmm."

"I meant milk."

"No. A man can't live on bread alone," I said, grinning in the darkness. "He withers."

"He won't," she said smugly. "Four more months."

"I wither at the very thought."

"Ann came three or four weeks early."

"Hurry this one."

"Don't you want a boy?" she asked then.

We'd discussed that before. I was well satisfied with Ann; it didn't matter to me if we had another girl. "Right now, I prefer girls ... lots of girls ... all kinds and shapes and ages," I said. "I leer at old ladies crossing streets."

She turned serious. "I'm sorry, Puppy."

"I was only joking, darling. You know that." I leaned over and kissed her. She smelled so clean and fresh, and her lips had a well-remembered passion.

Then Ann woke up, and I went into her room. I carried her into the bathroom, her little head sleepily on my shoulder. In the bathroom, she turned to look up at the sky. "There are no stars tonight, Daddy, because the fog is there."

"Yes, dear," I murmured.

"Daddy, is the sky blue?"

"Yes, dear."

"Then why are the stars white? Why aren't the stars blue when night comes?"

"Stars aren't part of the sky, darling. Stars are in the sky— swimming there like fish."

That satisfied her. She kissed me when I tucked her in.

By the time I got back to my bed, I was aglow with happiness and pride. I was thinking about Ann and Sue, already asleep beside me. Before I knew it, I was asleep, too—and not thinking about the centipede anymore.

Sunday I went over to the children's amusement park on La Cienega and Beverly, where a lot of other fathers tried unsuccessfully to conceal their pride. Ann rode on everything, as long as she liked—because she always comes without a murmur when it's time to go home. It's funny to watch those kids in the little automobiles, going around and around, their solemn little faces showing no pleasure, no excitement.

Then I wasn't amused. Because it struck me that I, too, was going around and around, solemnly, with no excitement.

But I brushed that thought away. Or hoped I did.

After dinner that night, Sue and I played two-handed pinochle, and she kept beating me. Which proved I wasn't concentrating— because she rarely beats me and never before ended up winning.

But it was a pleasant, quiet evening. My mind was still, congealed.

All day Monday, it stayed that way. I didn't work. I told Kate to stay home. It was a bad day, I explained. One of these no-work days. I have them from time to time.

Tuesday morning I had to get a haircut at Rothschild's. So I happened to be driving down Wilshire. And it was a lovely day, and I had the top down, and a lot of time to spare before my appointment with the barber.

I drove down to Mac's beat, below Doheny.

I pretended it was going to be a casual meeting, just like the others I'd had with him. Just to gab. And maybe he wouldn't be around, anyway. That would be a good sign; it would mean I'd better not speak to him. There was a car about a block ahead of me, and I stepped on the gas to overtake it. If the license number added up to an even number, I'd go on and see him. If it was an odd number, I'd turn around and go to the barbershop.

It added up to an odd number. So I tried the next car. That one was even. That meant I'd drive down to Doheny.

He wasn't there. I drove around for quite a while, but didn't see the police car. I waited until I was almost late for the barber, and then turned back.

Barney gave me his usual excellent haircut; and it's not easy to do a symmetrical job on close-cropped straight hair. Other barbers make me look as if I'd been decapitated recently. While he was snipping away with the scissors, I remember wishing he could snip closer and closer and get at that centipede. But he didn't.

After I left the barbershop, I drove back to Doheny, wondering if I'd see him this time, figuring that if I did, it was meant to be. Sure. Kismet. Kismet and a biological urge.

This time he was there.

Those police cars seem to slip up on tiptoes like your conscience. One minute I was alone, looking for him; the next, he had cut in on my right and pulled up beside me.

We pulled up in front of the Fox-Wilshire Theatre. It was early in the day and the box office was closed.

I got into the police car with him.

"Who scalped you, boy?" he said quietly.

I rubbed my hand over my hair. "I do feel kind of naked," I said. "How're things, Mac?"

"Slow. But no complaint," he said. "Heard from Fred lately?"

"Talked to me the other day. I think I told you about that. Not since then."

I noticed that the numbers on the 'wanted car' list had changed, but not very much. 'George Moreno' was still wanted, his photo a constant reminder on the dashboard. But another had been added to it—a square-faced solid man. 'Robert T. Villiers, alias R.

T. de Ville, alias Roy T. Varney, alias R. Theodore Vincent.' Mac had once told me that not more than one man in a thousand ever abandoned his initials when he took an alias.

"Another purse snatcher?" I said, pointing at the new one.

He looked at me. "No. Breaking and entering. We've been after him for a long time. Four successful jobs in town, and all we had was the outside third of a pinky print. And we weren't sure of that."

"How do you know he's the one?"

"Mostly on M.O.," he said. Then he saw my question coming. "M.O. is modus operandi—the method a criminal uses in committing a crime. There's an M.O. Bureau in Sacramento, with a file of all the methods ever used—pass keys, jimmies, metal workers, celluloid men …"

"What's a celluloid man?"

"Well, he uses a thin piece of celluloid, bent and worked to fit the shape of a door jamb. You slip it through and around, pull back, and it snaps the lock open." His head turned slightly as he watched a couple of girls go by. They were wearing yellow slacks, tight, and thin black sweaters through which you could see the neat lines of brassiere.

He went on. "This guy had another trick. He only took houses on the corner. Every time. So he could keep an eye on two streets, and see if a car approached. Another thing. The minute he enters a house, he goes to the front door and jams a kitchen match into the lock. If anybody comes home while he's working, he's got a five-minute warning. You come home, take out your key, and it doesn't fit into the lock. You keep trying. Then you spend a few minutes getting the match out. By that time, he's a half a mile away."

"He's got something," I said.

Mac nodded. "Clean job, every time. But after we spotted the M.O. we called on the M.O. Bureau in Sacramento. They checked, and said an ex-con, two years out of San Quentin, named Villiers, used the corner-house trick, and the match in the lock. We got his prints; and it matched our piece of pinky print." He indicated the photograph. "We'll pick him up now."

Just the fact that he was so relaxed and calm shouldn't have irritated me. But it did. Because I wasn't calm. Hardly hearing his story about the corner-house con—the kind of story I usually like to hear from him—I was eyeing him, trying to get to him, trying to pigeonhole him in my mind. A few little items registered—the thick hair on his wrist, the Patek wristwatch with the black leather band, and his big comforting bulk. Yes, comforting. You felt safe with him. You felt all cops ought to be that massive and self-assured and kindly. Dignity that came not only from his uniform but from his gray-at-the-temples good looks made me less fearful of what might happen to the Smiley woman.

That morning he was more within the frame of his background—a fairly wealthy family in Colorado, a civil engineer, and a wife ... Yes, a wife somewhere. Fred had told me about that. Nothing in particular had broken them up. As Fred put it, "she just got sick of being the wife of a cop." Maybe she discovered in him a few of the things I was beginning to detect.

Anyway, we talked some more. But not for long. He had kept the motor running this time, and he didn't call the central bureau and take time out. He didn't get a call while I was with him, but he finally said he had to make one.

I started to get out. When the door slammed, I looked inside, off-hand. "Anything new on the Smiley woman?"

"No." He was in gear now, looking back to see if the road was clear.

What made me say it? I don't know. All along, the words were waiting in my throat, as if they knew when to come out, the way gophers do.

"Got her number?" I asked.

He reached into his breast pocket and pulled out a slip of paper. I took it.

"All ready for you," he said. "Let me know."

He pulled away from the curb and I just stood there looking after him. What made him so sure I was going to ask for it? What made him so sure?

Cars were thickening the traffic when I got back to Beverly Hills—the noontime crowd. I stopped off for lunch at a little lunchroom near Santa Monica Boulevard. Somehow, I didn't feel

like going home. I was uneasy, restless, and a little bit guilty—
as if I were already unfaithful.

The telephone number was burning a hole in my pocket. While
I had my lunch, I took it out and put it beside my plate. A
Crestview number—1-6343. I didn't want to carry it around
with me, not home, anyway; that would be like bringing another
woman into the house. So I memorized the number, trying to hit
on an association. It totaled seventeen; so did my house number.
I tore up the paper.

After that, it kept burning a hole in my head.

And I didn't like being so scared. It hurt my male vanity. I felt
like a Milquetoast.

I tried to comfort myself. After ten years of marriage, you grow
cautious, that's all. Even though I was ashamed of being so tense
and timid just because I had memorized a phone number, I
realized it was natural. After a few years, you lose the spirit of
adventure; you're scared of it.

But, after all, Mac was cautious, too. He wouldn't put himself
in a position where he could be shaken down. But he wasn't
scared, either. He had made a decision; he wouldn't stop. That
neat clear policeman's-report handwriting—Crestview 1-6343.
Definite. Purposeful.

That's the way he dealt with Fred's divorce a couple of years ago.
Fred's wife was a beautiful girl, and she spread her beauty far and
wide. Damned near everybody in the picture business knew
about her; except Fred. It finally got to Mac, who wasn't even
connected with Hollywood at that time; he was working
downtown. He was the one who told Fred about it. But he didn't
get anywhere. Fred was furious, said he had a cop's mind and he
carried it low. But the suspicion flowered nicely, especially since
Mac made it his business to keep a check on the girl and report
her various activities. Fred didn't want to listen; but whenever the
phone rang, he answered it—and got an earful. He squirmed and
fought because he didn't want to hear and he didn't want to
believe. After a while, he *knew*; and still he wouldn't believe. But
Mac kept pounding away. She was taking him for a sleigh ride;
he was a sucker; he was paying for someone else's piper.

Fred never even questioned her. He didn't want to know. But

Mac wouldn't stand for it. So he picked one of her regular boyfriends, staked out the house, and then planted a dictagraph. He made seven records in the upstairs bedroom and one, the worst one, in the living room. It was there in sound; everything. The change in the tone of voice, the excitement, the urgency, the whimpering, the words, the terrible words Fred had never heard her speak—foul and feverish. You could even hear the sound of a zipper.

Then he took the records over to Fred's apartment and played them for him on a fine high-fidelity gramophone. He made Fred listen. Held him down. Fred got away and locked himself in the bathroom, but Mac shoved the gramophone right up against the bathroom door and turned the volume up high. It was plenty high—it got through the door, reverberated in the bathroom, got through Fred's hands, into his ears, and right into his bones.

Fred's alone now.

But that's Mac for you. And don't think that was cruelty. He knew Fred would suffer more if it dragged on and on; and he wouldn't permit a friend of his to take it that way. He went into action. Of course, not very delicately. He's a cop. He did it like a cop. Maybe that's the only way he knows. But he knew what would work on Fred.

And he evidently knew what would work on me. He had had that number ready for me.

I showed plenty of resistance that afternoon. Without even speaking to Sue or Kate, I went into the den when I got home. The script was on the desk, and I worked on it all afternoon. There was no need to push; the scenes flowed, the people came alive, and the dialogue was right.

Ann has learned not to interrupt me when I'm working, but from time to time she comes in on tiptoe and asks to kiss me, to be sure I love her. "I love you all the time," she says. That's her way of expressing the ultimate in love. All the time.

Other than that, there were no interruptions. Kate took the revised pages home with her for retyping, and after dinner I went back to work. Almost a week's work was crowded into those few hours.

At about eleven o'clock I went into the kitchen for a coke. I brought it back to the den, put it down, picked up the phone and dialed. Crestview 1-6343. The coke felt sharp; from too much smoking. Three buzzes in the phone. Four. No answer?

Then a voice said, "Hello?"

Up until then I could see what I was doing. Every movement I made was reasonable. I was a guy making a phone call.

But I didn't know what number I had dialed. I didn't know. And when that voice came over, I was panicked. I just stood there, while her voice said, "Hello? Hello? Hello?"

After a moment, she hung up. But I didn't. There was no sound on the wire. "Hello, Mrs. Smiley," I said absently.

The whole thing was stupid. Upstairs that night, just lying there, it made me feel sick and foolish to think about it. I was unprepared. "Unprepared." The way I used to say it at college when the prof called on me and I'd been out all night before. "Unprepared."

What was I going to say? Hello, Mrs. Smiley, how about my coming over and crawling in with you? It was stupid! Where did I get her number? Who was I, and why was I calling? What did I want?

It was fortunate Sue was asleep. She would have heard me. I was so incensed, I must have whispered a few words into the darkness. Unprepared. Script not ready. Incomplete.

Acting like a kid at the mushy poetry stage, acting like a wolf with his tail between his legs. It was undignified. it was ignominious!

Maybe it was. But the anger took the place of the hesitancy. It seems perfectly plain now that the reason I'd been able to work that day was that I had finally made a decision.

The centipede walked softly now.

CHAPTER 3

Next morning there was nothing to do but wait. When I left the bedroom, Sue was still asleep. The phone is on my side of the bedroom and the short cord doesn't reach all the way to her. Usually I put the phone on my bed; she can reach it then. But she's still not allowed to move, so I knew she wouldn't pick it up if it rang and woke her.

And there wasn't a chance that it wouldn't ring. Some parts of Mac's character were pretty clear by now—a certain pattern of behavior, a certain cause and effect, reason followed by inevitable action.

He phoned, all right.

Kate hadn't arrived yet, and I had closed the doors in the den. I had the receiver up before the first ring was halfway through.

"Jon? How'd it go?"

"How *would* it go?" I snapped. "I rang her and I didn't even speak to her. I had to hang up. I had nothing to say."

"Why not?"

"Oh, hell! How do I know her? Where did I get her number? What do I want? She can't read our minds. And if she did, she'd flush 'em with Lysol."

He chuckled at me. That forced heartiness they use when they're interrogating someone. We're your friends. Sure. We want to help you. That's all. We're here to protect you.

"God, you're a baby," he said then. "Just tell her you're a friend of her husband's …"

I stopped him. "I've never even seen the guy."

"All right, you're a friend of a friend of his. Let's say Smiley has a friend named Barnes, Ted Barnes. This Barnes is a fat guy, about five-feet-ten, brown hair and …"

"Okay, okay. What about him?"

"Barnes is a friend of yours. He knew you'd be lonesome coming out to California and not knowing anybody. So he told you to look up the Smileys."

I was clicking now, hearing myself telling her this over the phone. "How did Barnes happen to have Smiley's address?"

"Smiley wrote him a letter."

It sounded good. Reasonable. Straight. "Wait a minute," I said then. "Suppose, right after I phone her, she goes over and talks to Smiley. He's going to say he doesn't know any Barnes, and he didn't write anybody named Barnes!"

He had that stacked, too. "Don't be worrying about things like that. Leave them to me," he said confidently. "I just won't let her into the jail to visit him for the next few days. I'll tell the boys to keep her out of there. When everything's set, we'll let her visit him again."

He had everything figured—from beginning to end, as it turned out.

"Okay, I'll try it."

"When?"

"This afternoon, maybe. Or tonight. Whenever I get around to it."

"Let me know."

"Sure."

I hung up. It was all set. You may fire when ready, Gridley.

It was about eleven o'clock that morning when I pulled the trigger.

Talking to her was like anticipating television by phone. Memory, like a radiotronic tube, scans your thoughts and your words and everything you've heard. It gave me an instantaneous picture. It furnished a living room in which she stood at the phone. It put a thin silk dress on her that clung to a body Mac had described as "like a jig's." It even dissolved the dress while she spoke.

"Hello," I said, "Mr. Smiley there?"

"Why, no. He's not in right now. Is there anything I can do? This is Mrs. Smiley." It was a voice charged with juice, and it made a contact with me.

"Well, I don't know, Mrs. Smiley. I just got in from the East. My name is Jon Forbes, and I'm a friend of a friend of Mr. Smiley's. Ted Barnes told me to look him up."

"Oh, I see. Well, he's not here now."

"When will he be back?"

She hesitated. "I don't know exactly. He's got a job in the movies and he's off on location."

"Oh, well, maybe I'd better call again in a few days."

Again the pause. "He'll be gone quite a while, I'm afraid."

"Oh. That's too bad. I don't know anybody out here, and I thought we could get together. Maybe have dinner or a few drinks."

I heard Sue ring the buzzer to the kitchen; she was awake, and ready for breakfast. There was still time to hang up, still time to back out.

"Well," the voice said, "that might be just the thing for me, Mr. Forbes. We don't know anybody out here yet, either. It's no fun being a stranger in town."

"No, it isn't," I said quickly, too quickly, it seemed to me. I was leaping at the bait like a famished flounder; and so was she. "I'd be very happy to meet you anywhere you like ..."

"I don't know many places in town."

"Neither do I," I said. "But maybe we can meet somewhere and search around for a place we like."

"Well ... Where are you staying, Mr. Forbes?"

That almost caught me. Where was I staying? What hotel was safe? "The Hotel Sackville," I said. "It's just a small place, and kind of depressing. Why don't we meet at that big hotel in Beverly Hills—the Beverly Wilshire? They have a nice bar."

"That will be fine. What time?"

"Say, about eight-thirty, tonight?"

"That's fine. I'll see you then."

"Good." I was about to hang up when her voice came through again.

"Wait a moment," she said, giggling. "How will I know you?"

I hadn't thought of that. Me, I knew her already. I could see her standing there talking to me. My hand was out to touch her.

"Oh, yes. That's right. We could have walked right by each other," I said. "How about telling the bartender where you're sitting, and then I'll come in and ask him. Or if I get there first, I'll do it."

She laughed again. "All right. See you then. Good-by."

"Good-by," I said. And hello, Mrs. Smiley. Hello at last.

Right after I hung up, I got into action. There was no way of contacting Mac, except by finding him in the police car. I had to get him to cover for me.

Telling Sue I was going over to my agent's office, I dashed out and got into the car. The car screeched as I backed it out under full power. To hell with speeding tickets; Mac could take care of that. I had to get to him quickly.

I raced up and down almost every street in his section of town, but I must have been a good distance behind him. I never caught up with him. Then I got worried for fear he might phone while I was out. So I hurried home again.

It was almost dinner time when he phoned. When he heard what had happened, he was very pleased.

"But what about the hotel?" I said. "Suppose she checks me at the Hotel Sackville and finds out I'm not registered there?"

"Why would she do that? You're a friend of her husband's. Why the hell should she check on you?"

"But suppose she does?"

"All right, all right. I'll see the clerk over there and he'll cover for you."

"That's better," I said. "I don't want to look like a damned fool …"

"Forget it, I'll call you tomorrow. Good luck."

"Thanks."

Good luck, he said. Sure. Godspeed. *Pax vobiscum.* Blessings. What he meant was: good hunting—bring her back.

But, in a way, I was lucky that afternoon. Because when I went to the studio, I felt as if I'd swallowed a handful of bennies. Lots of writers take Benzedrine tablets for stimulation. Almost thirty pages of script were done by five o'clock. Good stuff that a director wouldn't have trouble with on the shooting stages; scenes that almost played themselves. Brawley read the copy before he left for the day, and I knew it was good. When he doesn't like something, he suggests that it could be improved. When it's fair, he says it's pretty good. When it's exactly right, he says it's excellent. This stuff was labeled excellent.

That left me feeling pretty good. First, because there was a feeling of accomplishment; second because my mind was clear to focus on what lay ahead.

With the first step taken, duplicity comes easily. You scheme and twist and turn. I know. The thirty pages left me clear for the night; I could tell Sue 1 was working very late. I knew that even while I was writing them. And I was looking way ahead of that. Before I phoned Sue to tell her I wasn't coming home to dinner, I made some preparations. Two packs of chewing gum—for my breath; a small can of cleaning fluid, for any lipstick that might get on my clothes; and a small bottle of Atkinson's Lavender Water, my favorite after-shave lotion, to counteract any perfume she might be using.

Oh, I was pretty shrewd. Everything was all set. Except me.

Walking into the lobby of the Beverly-Wilshire, I realized I'd made my first mistake. It was the first place I'd been able to think of. But it was lousy with picture people. Three of them waved hello before I'd passed the elevators.

The walk toward the bar was like the last mile. But by that time I could see through the glass partitions into the bar. I could see the bartender.

Without looking around, I walked up to the bar and sat down. The place was jammed. Lighting a cigarette, shifting around on the bar stool, I covered the room. Way back in a booth there was a woman, alone.

One quick look was enough. Plenty. Descriptions of electrocutions say that the condemned man usually strains forward against the leather straps when the first shock hits him. That's the way I sat there. For half an hour afterward you could have put terminals anywhere on my body and lighted a small city.

Bartenders always stand in front of you, waiting. This one waited quite a while.

"Don't turn your head and don't point. Is that Mrs. Smiley back there in the corner booth?"

"Yeah," he said,

My wallet was out, and I slipped him five bucks. "Nobody asked for her," I said.

He nodded. "Nobody did."

I walked right out of the bar, around the corner to Rodeo Drive, and just kept walking.

Scared? Sure I was. But not because of the people who had recognized me in the lobby; and not because of the couple of men who nodded to me in the bar. It was something else. Premonition. Conscience. Something like that.

But I walked around Beverly Hills for an hour, counting my steps for each block, counting the trees, looking into those plate-glass windows in the bungalows. It was cold, but windless. The living rooms along Rodeo were drab Spanish affairs mostly, yellow bulbs shining against bilious plaster walls; and they were damned poor recommendations for domestic felicity. Outside, it was dark and too quiet. But there was a warm and lively bar up the block. The Beverly-Wilshire Bar. Comfortable; good liquor; and high voltage in a corner booth.

I went home.

Oh, I felt virtuous—and smug; and ashamed of myself. Ashamed of myself for not going through with it. But I was home early; presumably because I wasn't able to work well. And when I'm tired like that, after working hard, Sue doesn't speak much to me. I got undressed and went into the bathroom. I opened the door of the right-hand medicine cabinet. A bottle of Atkinson's Lavender Water was on the bottom shelf.

I put my robe back on and went into the bedroom. "I'm going to make some notes," I said. "Be right back."

"Don't be long, darling," Sue said. "You look tired."

Sure. Tired. Not too tired to pick up the phone. I knew the upstairs extension was out of Sue's reach again.

But she'd left the bar. Almost an hour ago. So I phoned her at home. She was there. I thought maybe someone else got her.

"Hello?" she said. Now the voice had a face behind it—not vague and tantalizing. But known, and more than tantalizing.

"Hello … This is Jon Forbes. I'm sorry. I got to the bar and you were gone. My car broke down. Please forgive me …"

"Oh … I *thought* something was wrong. At first I wondered if I had the right bar …"

"You had the right one. I was just unlucky enough to have a flat

… and no jack … And of course, I don't know my way around."

There was a pause. "No. I guess you don't …" She paused again. "Did you get a garageman?"

"Yes. I'm all set now … Will you let me make it up to you tomorrow night?"

"Yes."

"Good. But meet me there at seven. Then we'll go to dinner."

"Fine …"

"Good-by."

"Good-by."

How can I tell you what the first sight of her did to me? Is there such a thing as a depraved virgin? Because she looked depraved and she looked virginal. And I only saw her from the neck up. It was in her eyes and in her lips, and in the taut way she held her head. Eyes gray and fathomless; and hair blacker than the polished belt Mac wore. The thought of him next to her hurt the way it hurts when you catch your finger in a car door.

Ask me how I got through the next day. Ask me. I didn't breathe. I didn't talk. I didn't eat. Or I don't know about it.

Sometime during the day, Mac phoned me. I didn't speak to him. I told Kate to tell him the date was changed to tonight. That was all.

I had lunch with four other writers, and I must have been in a daze because, when I looked up one time, they had emptied their pockets of all their Benzedrine tablets and piled them up in front of me. About two dozen of them.

"Take 'em all," someone said. "You're sluggy."

Later I found out I didn't even pay my check for lunch, and when Brawley spoke to me as I was walking out, I didn't even hear him.

But writers are acknowledged screwballs, and nobody made much of it. I was just having a bad day.

How bad, even I didn't know.

CHAPTER 4

That night I walked into the bar through the side entrance. Right up to the bar. Casual. Waving to a writer from Metro. Just having a drink. And all the while I was at the bar, I could feel her looking at me. I hadn't seen her, but I knew she was in the same booth and I knew she was watching me.

The bartender, the same one, seemed surprised, but he played along. He nodded his head toward the rear booth. I turned around, and from there on I felt like a cinch for a Barnum & Bailey contract—because I walked a tightrope all the way to the rear booth, and the rope was strung between a couple of stars. Why does it have to make sense? That's the way it was!

I looked down at her. "Hello, I'm ..."

"Yes, I know."

Moving in opposite her, I held on to her hand, then dropped it quickly.

"I hope I didn't keep you waiting," I said. I hope I wasn't late; I wish I'd been early; I wish I'd been here years ago.

She shook her head. "I just arrived."

The waiter came over and we ordered two scotches—Pinch bottle. It seems everybody does. Over in Europe, crème de menthe is known as the whore's drink; they all sit at cafe tables with that green drink in front of them. Over here, almost every time you see a couple squeezed into a corner as if nobody could see them, they're drinking scotch and soda. Maybe they're just not thinking about what they're drinking. I know I wasn't. I drank the stuff, but it could have been sheep-dip for all I knew.

"I'm sorry about last night," I said.

She looked up, eyes wide. "What happened?"

"My car broke down and ..."

"What happened?" she said. No change of tone. She just ignored my explanation.

"My car broke down," I said. Nobody could believe it, said like that.

"Liar," she said softly.

"But look, Mrs. Smiley, I ..."

She shook her head. "I saw you come in and speak to the bartender." She paused then, "Didn't you like my looks?"

There wasn't any need to answer that. Just the way I looked at her must have answered. She wore a green dress, the shade of spring leaves, and around her thin neck there was a gold chain made up of a series of hearts, small ones. Over her left breast she had a beautifully wrought piece of costume jewelry. It was a small gold trapeze, and on it sat a little gold man in tights. She kept playing with it, and the man turned over and over, attached to the crossbar.

That's what was happening to me, too; turning over and over, falling through the gray infinity of her eyes the way you do in a dream—never hitting bottom, just falling and turning and accelerating. And once in a while, like the man on the little trapeze, I'd bounce off that left breast that was meant for the cup of my hand.

I kept looking at her, and her lips parted a bit. Her teeth were small and sharp-looking.

"What was it, then?" she asked.

I looked away.

"Why'd you wait? Why'd you come back tonight?" I said. Any answer she made would have satisfied me. Loneliness. Curiosity. The fact that I was a friend of her husband's.

"Because you ran away," she said. "You were scared."

That hit, all right. "Why would I be scared?" I said, carefully. "You don't look that dangerous."

She smiled a little then. "How do you know?"

"I don't. Are you?"

She grinned suddenly, like a kid—with a mischievous, gleeful spread to her mouth. "Do you want to find out?"

I nodded. "I want to find out."

She looked at me a moment, and I felt as if I were blushing. I wasn't sure. But it felt like it. So I looked down at her hand, holding the glass of scotch. Most men never notice, but there are a dozen pretty faces for every pair of lovely hands. She had long fingers, almost without knuckles, just the merest definition of them. The skin looked as if it had no pores.

Those hands could touch you the way only dreams touch you—
deep inside; the kind of dreams from which you awaken drugged
and troubled and exhausted, returned from a long journey that
was so terrible and ecstatic that there's never any remembrance
of it.

Then she spoke, and that dream was over; but I was in another
one.

"Look," she said suddenly, "I'm hungry. But before we go out to
eat, let's make with some brass tacks." She didn't say it
belligerently at all. It was kind of apologetic.

"I'm fresh out of them, Mrs. Smiley."

"Mona," she said.

"Mona," I repeated.

"What's your name?"

I didn't get it. "Jon," I said, surprised. "Jonathan called Jon …
J—O—N."

"Is that really it?"

I still didn't get it. "What makes you think it isn't?"

"I don't know," she said, pulling out a compact. "This isn't my
type of game, at the moment. You see, I thought it might be
something else. Because right after you phoned the other day, I
phoned back to call it off. You aren't registered at the Hotel
Sackville."

A sandbag couldn't have left me more stunned. I just watched
her in amazement. She was looking into her compact mirror,
putting on some lipstick. Maybe you've never noticed, but that's
about the sexiest thing a woman can do without taking her
clothes off.

You can see the way her lips will part when you're kissing her.
You can see the way her mouth will shape itself in passion. And
when she flicks her tongue over her lips, you can read your
future in it.

Still watching her, I leaned back, letting go of the glass that was
clutched in my hand. "Why didn't you call it off?"

"I liked your voice."

It didn't make sense, and now it began to amuse me. I felt more
secure, knowing there was a response from her, knowing that this
wasn't entirely one-sided. I was sure of that.

"I've got one more tack left, right now," she said. "I don't think you know my husband, or anyone else who knows him. Never mind the explanations. Maybe we'll get to them later. But I just wanted you to know."

The smile on my face broadened and broadened until it began to hurt. Then that impish look came over her face—friendly, warm, as if she were giggling inside.

"Now let's go," she said then. "And stop looking at me as if you were going to eat me."

"Am I?"

She started getting up. "I don't know yet."

This time she wasn't smiling. She walked out lithely, like an animal—just as Mac said.

Why did I guide her through the lobby when we could have gone right through the rear door of the bar? There's no telling how many people recognized me as we passed through.

But I wanted to see her walk. I wasn't thinking of anything else. How can you think when you feel that way—with a warm rush of laughter wanting to come up in your throat? With a high note wanting to come out of you and shatter the chandeliers?

Every bit of furniture in the lobby was an obstacle because my eyes stayed on her—sideways. Watching her legs, watching the way she swayed, watching the way she walked on thick carpets even when she was on the marble floor. All right—how many women have you seen who walk on high heels as if they were stilts, wobbling sometimes, turning ankles, or being ungainly? Think about it and you'll know what I mean.

Mona walked like an animal.

When we got into my car, my mood had changed. I was rocketing. Just holding her arm as I helped her in, just feeling her slim forearm through her neat cloth coat, made me grin with pleasure.

Throwing it into first, I gave her a quick glance. "Did I say I was pleased to meet you?"

"No."

"Well, I am," I said. Then, softly, "Hello, Mona."

"Hello."

"I'm pleased to meet you because you're delightful. You're

wonderful!"

"No, I'm not. I'm a pretty woman you've just met. I'm married and my husband isn't around," she said simply.

How do you handle a woman like that? How do you keep your head? It was like hearing a '311' call on Mac's police radio. Indecent exposure. And she was exposing me.

Making a right turn, I managed to catch the look on her face, with a street light showing her little straight nose wrinkled and that wood sprite grin.

"And how do *you* do?" she said. There was the merest suggestion of laughter in her voice.

"Badly, at the moment."

"I wouldn't say that. I'm *here*," she said. "That's what you wanted, isn't it?"

She had me tongue-tied again. She kept beating me to the punch and reading me like a book.

"Turn the page," I said. "What else do you know about me?"

"Not enough."

"Want to hear more now?"

"No. I'm happy. I'm glad to be with you. Now let's find a restaurant."

It was breathtaking. She kept kicking me in the stomach with that direct talk and that elfish look; but every time she kicked me, I went higher and higher.

"Where'll we go?" I said.

"You name it," she said. Then added quickly, "And don't say you're a stranger in town. You know your way around."

Speechless again, I just drove on.

"Well, don't look so flabbergasted," she said. "After all, at least two people nodded to you when you were at the bar. Nobody nodded to me—because nobody in town knows me."

"Nobody nodded to you because they were all paralyzed. They were speechless, like me."

"You were speechless, but you weren't paralyzed. You ran like a scared rabbit." Then her voice softened. "Now, don't get that look. I didn't mean to hurt you."

"It's all right. I *was* scared."

"Why?"

I didn't answer.

"Why?"

I just kept driving.

"I was, too, you know."

Now it was my turn. "Why?"

"Oh, you're such a fool! Can't I speak out with you? Can't you be honest?" she snapped. "I got it from your voice over the phone. I got it when I looked at you at the bar. We click; we spark. You know it and I know. Now for God's sake let's eat; I'm starving!"

I'd put out my hand to catch a lamb, and right before my eyes it turned into a tigress. But such a sleek, lovely one.

Down on Western, below Wilshire, there was a fine restaurant that was fairly secluded. I'd found it once on the way back from San Pedro. The food was good, and the patrons weren't from Hollywood or the picture business.

We had a booth and a certain amount of privacy. And there was a little light on top of the partition, shining down so that her hair looked blue-black and gleaming. She wore a little green box of a hat that looked crazy to me; but it must have been chic because every woman who saw it looked envious. As far as I was concerned she could have worn a double boiler.

I felt silly. I beamed at the waiter when he smiled approvingly at her. I wanted everybody to see her and admire her. I wanted everybody to know how wonderful she was.

Then she pointed at my food. "Eat that—not me," she said.

After a moment, she smiled. "You'll be hungry later."

"Sometimes, the way you move your lips, the way you smile, the way your eyes change—they speak so loudly, I can't hear what you're saying." That was me; groggy.

She looked down at her food.

"You know," I said, "it must be my lucky star that does these things to me. Or maybe it's because I didn't get much for Christmas. You're my Christmas package."

She kept looking down, not eating now, just listening.

"Hey," I said, "you're my Christmas package and I haven't even opened you yet." Now I was whispering. "But even the outside of the package is wonderful."

"Don't," she said. Looking up, her face was virginal and very young, so young that I was touched. It made her reach deeper inside me. It hurt.

That was when I had to look down, my eyes tracing the little design around the plate.

"Jon," she said softly.

"What?"

"How are you fixed for scruples?"

For a minute, I thought I had only heard it in my head; me talking to me. When I looked up, she was playing with the little trapeze-artist pin, whirling him around and around on the bar.

I pointed at it. "You're doing that to me." Then, since she was waiting for me to take it from there, I couldn't switch. "Why?"

She shrugged. "Because I've just become a mother. Up here," she said, pointing to her forehead.

It sounded screwy, but her face was solemn.

"He's a little old man with a beard," she went on. "He looks something like those cartoons of Mr. Prohibition. And he's marching up and down in my mind, picketing me."

"A little thing called conscience?"

She nodded.

I tapped my head with a forefinger. "Have him say 'hello' to his brother over here," I said.

"*Two* of them?" she asked hopelessly.

I nodded.

This was a hell of a time to bring that up. It was like bringing down a bird on the wing, stopped in midflight and then tumbling down.

"Maybe we can kill them," I said.

"They die hard."

"We'll throttle them," I said. "Or poison them. Or, better still, they'll burn to a crisp when we touch each other."

She didn't answer. But while we drank our coffee, you could almost hear the click of adding machines as we drew up balance sheets of "do" and "don't."

My little man was guarding that house in Beverly Hills and ten years of what the world regards as safety. All right, what was *her* little man guarding? A purse snatcher, a punk kid who probably didn't even know what he had.

Oh, sure; it was easier that way; attacking her position instead of examining my own. But by that time I was past self-criticism. By that time there was only the fragrance of her, the curve of her neck; the shock of her directness; and the sum total of all that I'd been thinking of her in the back of my head since first I heard about her.

We weren't looking at each other now. But when I leaned forward with my hand under the table, I found hers waiting. Smooth as a child's hand, it was; the bones felt soft ... soft ... soft ... The sounds in the restaurant would come up suddenly in waves, and then recede and let our breathing become plain to both of us. A kid came in with the evening papers. But he took one look at us, whistled softly, and didn't even try to sell us one.

Sure, it was adolescent, and it must have looked ridiculous. But nobody who feels it will ever give a damn about how it looks. Nobody at the climax ever closes his mouth because he may not look presentable.

"Bill is sweet," she said finally, as if pleading with me to understand her. "He's very young, and he loves me. And I'm married to him ..."

When I looked up, a change had come over her face. First a look of discovery, then comprehension, and then a touch of bitterness. She wasn't looking at me when she continued.

"But I didn't realize until now that I never liked him."

Outside, it had begun to rain, driving down in a hard slanted stream. We didn't hurry to get into the car; we just walked along, almost slow motion. After we got in, we sat there silently. The ignition key was still in my hand. Mona stayed far over on the other side.

The no-draft window on my side was out of trim, and water seeped in rhythmically, like a pulse beat, and then dropped off to the floor. On the canvas top, the rain drummed steadily.

"I don't know whether I meant that," Mona said. "I'm not sure I dislike Bill. You're making me dislike him."

Pulling out my cigarettes, I held them toward her. She took one, and when the glow from my lighter hit her face, she was watching me. Her eyes and eyebrows slanted upward; that's what gave her the elfin look.

When the top of the lighter snapped shut, I was facing her, watching the white of her teeth and the shape of her lips in the glow of a street lamp. It reminded me of how dainty she was. No bloody smears of lipstick on napkins; not even on that little paper napkin in the Beverly-Wilshire bar. Fastidious. The rain drops on her hat and coat didn't belong there.

She reached forward, looking for the ash tray, and her hand touched the glove compartment. I grabbed her hand quickly, and directed it toward the ash tray. It was a quick, odd action. What was in the glove compartment but some gum, a bottle of Atkinson's Lavender Water, and a can of cleaning fluid? What's wrong with them? Nothing; but I would have cut my arm off before I let her see them.

The little beads of rain, catching the street lights, moved down the windshield like tiny glowworms. I put the key in and started. The windshield wipers cleaned the outside; but the inside was foggy with smoke and our breaths. Very foggy.

I pulled out my handkerchief and cleared a space. Right across the way I saw a policeman, in helmet cover and raincoat, trying a door. Where do they get their raincoats when a quick storm comes up? That's what bothered me. I kept thinking about that as I drove out.

That was something else I'd have to talk to Mac about.

All the way up to Carthay Circle we didn't speak. There was a kind of tension between us, and a silence that was like the modesty that comes over two people who see each other naked for the first time. We didn't look at each other.

"You smell good," I said, after a while.

"Thank you." An adolescent voice, a troubled voice.

"What is it?"

"Tigress. Inexpensive, but ... *you* like it."

I made a very bad joke of it. "Tigress," I said, "but a pussy cat's wearing it."

She threw me a look out of a corner of her eye. "And a rabbit's sniffing it," she said curtly.

There we were, in sight of the Fox-Wilshire Theatre, rolling closer to wherever she lived, and all we had in mind was a couple of little old men picketing our minds.

"Where do you live?"

"On Spaulding ..."

It had stopped raining. The windshield wipers seemed to be slowing down, groaning against the drying glass just as the conversation was groaning. I shut them off.

Turning down Spaulding, I felt empty and limp. After a while, she pointed. "Over there," she said.

It was an apartment house like many others, I suppose. To me, it was an inaccessible citadel, guarded by little old men, picketing. It was bathed in glory like one of those motion picture trick shots showing the dead walking through knee-deep clouds to a great beyond streaming with sunrays. Maudlin, maybe; romanticizing, maybe; but it made me feel hollow inside.

"Which one is it?" I asked.

"The front one, on the left."

"The lights are on."

"Yes," she said, "Claire must be there."

I looked at her in surprise. "Who's Claire?"

"Claire Garner. She and her husband came out from New York with us," she said. Then she giggled softly. "They must be friends of that friend of yours, too. The one who told you to look us up."

There was no answer to that one, either. I didn't want to go into it. But what was Claire Garner doing there? She was the wife of Smiley's purse-snatching partner. But did she live there?

"Does she stay with you?"

"No. She just gets lonely at her place and sometimes spends the night with me. Her husband's away, too," Mona said. Then after a pause, "I didn't think it would make any difference tonight. So when she asked to come, I let her."

I shut off the motor and turned off the headlights. Out came the cigarettes again. Maybe they'd keep her with me a while longer.

"How do you feel?" she said then.

"Fine. Except that someone seems to have stolen my Christmas present."

"I feel low, too."

Her hand was on the seat, and mine touched it. I raised it and kissed her palm, and then the pinky, touching it lightly with my tongue. She trembled. You can do lots of things with a hand. She began to lean toward me.

"Don't," she said.

"Why?"

"Because I like it."

Tigress, like the perfume she wore; that was tigress' logic. But I let her take her hand away.

"Will you phone me tomorrow?" she asked.

"What for?" If this was the way it was to be, there was no sense to it.

"Because I want you to. And because you want to," she said quietly. "In the morning?"

"I don't know. I'll be busy tomorrow."

"What do you do?"

"I'm a writer. Studio."

"What've you written?"

I named a couple of books I'd written, and a few pictures. She kept watching my face while I spoke, as if she were trying to make sure I wasn't lying.

"Have you been using your professional dialogue tonight?" she said, grinning again.

"I was going to," I admitted. "But none of it fit. I had to ad lib all evening. It was kind of unexpected ..."

"What was?"

It was hard to say. "I don't know ... I ... just didn't expect to be hit this way."

Her voice was low, a deep whisper almost. "I hope you mean that. Because it goes double."

Then I leaned toward her. "Tigress, Tigress, burning bright, in the forest of the night ..."

But she turned away.

"I haven't even kissed you," I said.

"I'd never get out of the car," she said, staring out the window. "I've got a very low boiling point."

She opened the door.

"Don't get out," she said. She rolled the window down, shut the door, and leaned on it, looking in at me.

Leaning across the seat, I looked up at her. All I could do was shake my head back and forth in wonder at what she did to me inside.

"I think you're going to have trouble with me, mister," she said softly. "And I think my little old man is headed for a marble slab."

She walked away, and I watched her as she walked into the apartment. She was outlined in the doorway for an instant, and then the door closed.

I was alone. I was more alone than I'd ever been in my life.

CHAPTER 5

As I drove home, it wasn't raining, but I could still hear a drumming sound on the canvas top. It was a drumming in my ears and in my pulse. And then as I came into Beverly, my mind cleared. Burton Way, Sunset, closer to home, closer to home.

The first thing that struck me was that nothing I had done that night could be construed as actual infidelity. Then why was I so nervous? Why did I feel cold all of a sudden? My brain began to click.

It was mechanical, mentally mechanical. Little wheels whirred, gears meshed, delicate scales weighed this and that eventuality; new machines and instruments, created in those past few days, delivered a considered course of action.

All recorded. The gum, lavender water, and cleaning fluid could remain in the glove compartment. I hadn't been close enough to her to have the odor of Tigress on me. No lipstick. Had I eaten at the studio? No; the commissary closed too early, and I'd already told Sue the lunchroom was run by the Borgias and I'd never eat there. All right; a drive-in. Yes. I was in a hurry and ate in a drive-in; then went back to work. What if Sue had phoned? Simple; I was in the men's room.

Anything else? No. Oh, yes: script. It didn't go well. I was tired. Report concluded.

But the report was useless. In my house it would always be useless. Because there was never a doubt, and there was consequently no interrogation. It was I who squirmed and schemed and connived, and I was brought up short when I realized the trust that lived in my house.

No, it wasn't Sue's voice that troubled me; it was Mona's. Mona's voice in my head.

When I slipped into bed, Sue was still reading. She heard me sigh.

"Didn't it go well tonight?" she asked. *"You were scared,"* Mona's *voice said.*

"No. And I'm wrecked."

"You always are when you don't work well. And then the next day you turn out a lot of stuff, and you feel fine," she said. "You always do." *"I'm here," Mona's voice said; "that's what you wanted, isn't it?"*

"Is Brawley bothering you?"

I shook my head. "Not yet." But Mona's bothering me; her voice. I could hear her saying it. *"How're you fixed for scruples?"*

"How was Ann today?" I said.

"Fine. She brought one of her paintings home from school. For you. You always get her treasures. It's on the dresser."

I got up and looked at it. A folded sheet of rough paper about three feet square. Unfolded, it was a child's mess of paint strokes, with a few well-defined ovals in black at the bottom. The rest was green streaks.

"What is it?" *"Tigress," Mona's voice said.*

"It's the ocean and some fish," Sue said, laughing. "She pointed out the big waves and the small waves. And, of course, there's a mommy fish, a daddy fish, and an Ann fish."

"The fish look all right," I said.

I folded the paper carefully and replaced it, and I knew I'd have to thank her for it at breakfast the next morning. Children bestow these gifts with infinite love and they must be acknowledged.

When I turned away from the bureau, I saw the carved teakwood figure of Buddha. It's part of the room, which has a Chinese motif. Two walls were painted a soft gray-blue. The other two were papered with what a decorator calls a "scenic." Chinese workmen plodded across delicate landscapes composed of artfully stunted trees, and a few fatly rounded huts stood on the rim of hills in the distance. The curtains were of glazed chintz, with the same scenes as the wallpaper. They come in sets. With the pagoda-shaped lamp-shades and the light-colored wood of the bureaus, night tables, and writing desk, it was a pleasing whole. And that Buddha was part of it. Chinese, delicate, laughing. A sleek, fat Buddha, with his hands raised ecstatically over his head and his blubbery breasts hanging limply. A talisman. He was the Buddha of Marital Happiness.

"Good night, Puppy," I said tonelessly.

We kissed.

"Good night, dear," Sue said.

And Mona's voice said, "I think you're going to have trouble with me, mister."

Guess who called next morning? Just casually; just to say hello; just to pass the time of day. Sure; Mac.

I hadn't been thinking about him much, but I'd been hating his guts since the moment I saw her. By this time, his quiet resonant voice grated on my nerves. He was a beefy blue vulture sitting on the green tile-and-gilt dome of the Beverly Hills courthouse, waiting for Mona. Waiting for me to bring her to him.

He asked me how it went, and I told him the date had been called off. It was for tonight. He said he had kept her from visiting Smiley yesterday and would do so again today. Not wanting to tell him that I'd already seen her, and that she knew I wasn't sent by any friend of Smiley's, I couldn't tell him he was needlessly depriving her of her right to visit. I had to let it go.

Then he encouraged me. I'd probably have no trouble. It was a cinch. She was hotter than a two-dollar pistol.

Someday you'll be able to spit in a guy's eye over the phone. I almost anticipated that day. How could he talk about her that way?

But I just gritted my teeth. I told him I'd talk to him the next day.

But you know what I thought then? Remembering what Mac had told me about dangerous juveniles, about kids hopped up with reefers and those barbiturate "goof balls," I thought maybe I wouldn't shed many tears if one of them blew his damned head off.

As soon as I got to the studio, I phoned her. And it was still the same. Just the sound of her voice tightened me up inside.

"Hello," I said. "I was afraid you wouldn't be home."

"I've been waiting all morning for you to call. Is that wrong?"

"No. Why should it be?"

"My mother always told me to be aloof … men like the chase …

be hard to get … be distant," she giggled. "I'm distant, all right. Just put out your hand."

My voice was husky. "I wish it could reach that far."

She sounded far away from the phone when she answered. "Let's pretend I didn't hear that."

But I kept on. "Little old man dead yet?"

She waited a moment. "Let's say he's ailing," she said. "And how's his brother?"

"Prognosis negative. May not live through the day," I said. "Let's hold a wake at your house tonight …"

It was only a second before she answered. One single second, but I went to hell and back again.

"I'm having dinner with Claire."

"And afterward?"

"Well, let's see," she said softly. "Then I'll take her home and I'll be back at my place at nine. And when I get to the door, you'll be waiting there. And I'll open the door and let you in."

"I'll let you precede me, of course; I know my manners," I said.

The sun was coming out; the rain was stopping. The stuff pouring down my office window at the studio was silver, pure silver, and I could go out and catch it in my hands.

"See that you do—after you're inside," she said then.

"Naturally. I never offend a lady."

Her voice was straightforward, as if she were talking to herself. Not joking; not solemn; but matter-of-fact.

"Since last night, I'm not sure I'm a lady. I think I'm a bitch. And I think you're glad of it."

And she hung up.

Brawley didn't call me; I called him. He never bothers a writer. Not like some producers, who keep snatching pages out of your typewriter, good or bad. Just so it's fast. Just so we can put the next man to work on it for the rewrite. Not Brawley. That's why his pictures have cohesion. That's why he's one of the top men in the industry, and one of these days will be *the* top man.

I told him I wanted to see him. With a man like that, you play it straight, because he understands.

He was sitting behind his desk, leaning back in the swivel

chair. Calm, attentive, courteous. He wears glasses, and he's rather thin, and his complete outfit doesn't run into the hundreds of dollars. He dresses simply, and he thinks straight. And I was a damned fool to think he wouldn't sense that something was radically wrong.

"I just wanted to tell you that I'm going to fall behind a bit," I said. "It's a personal matter bothering me and I can't work ... But when I get straightened out, it'll come lots faster. I've got the scenes and the people but ..."

"Anything I can help you with?"

"No. I'm afraid not. Thanks."

"Want to talk about it?"

He didn't have to say it would be confidential.

When I didn't answer, he frowned a moment. "When you want to talk about it, let me know. You can get me at home any time." He meant it, too. Because he knew I liked and respected him, and I knew he had a feeling for me, too.

I started out. "I just wanted to tell you about it before you began wondering," I said.

He nodded. "Why don't you take a few days off?"

"No thanks. I'm afraid I'd take advantage of that. I'd rather keep pushing, but not under pressure."

"That's all right," he said. "Holler when you're ready. It's going along fine."

It relieved me to get that over with.

Before I went out to dinner, I went to the Finlandia Baths. It wasn't intentional, but after I'd phoned Sue to tell her I wasn't coming home, after I'd talked to Ann over the phone and promised to take her to the zoo on Sunday, after that husband-and-father intimacy, I felt unclean. Nervous, too. Impatient. And I was walking into the steam room before I knew what I was doing.

The heat hit me the way Mona hit me—suffocating and warm to the bone. Starting at the lower beach, I worked my way to the top where the heat crushed you like a power press. After a little while, there wasn't enough energy in me to propel me to the bucket of water that beckoned from below a mile of stepped-down benches. Relaxed and dazed, I floated in hot clouds, and the perspiration began to drip off me.

I made it back to the floor by taking one bench at a time. Then Sam, the masseur, got to work on me, rubbing my body with coarse salt. I began to wake up.

Rub hard, rub hard with the rich salt, again and again. Bring forth the frankincense and myrrh, and still not the lutes that play so sweetly in mine ears. Deck me in gold raiment and let the perfumes of Araby be sprayed upon my body. Prepare me for the nuptials, for the Queen is waiting.

That's the way I felt until the ice-cold shower hit me. Then I went out to eat.

Naturally, it was long before nine o'clock when I parked in front of her apartment house and leaned back to wait. The lights were switched off, and I put the ignition key in my pocket. Twice I looked into the glove compartment; everything was there.

After fifteen minutes or so, it began to rain again. It could have rained andirons for all I cared. It bothered me only because I had to lean across the seat to watch her door through the wet window.

Then when I looked back up the street for the hundredth time, I saw her. She was wearing one of those transparent Pliofilm raincoats with a peaked hood. She looked nunlike, and the rain drops on the white robe picked up the street light and made her sparkle with the kind of radiance you see behind Madonnas in Italian paintings.

I walked up to her door and waited in the rain. She saw me, but she didn't hurry. I stepped out of her way when she pulled out the key. She opened the door, reached inside, and switched on the lights.

"Come into my parlor, said the spider ..." she murmured.

She walked toward the closet, taking her raincoat off. I put my coat down on a chair, but she came for it and hung it up. I sat down in an armchair and watched her.

She had done her hair differently. It was up-swept, severe over her ears, and it rose into an elaborate roll that was like a black coronet. Very few women can bear that severity without losing something. But she looked beautiful, regal, and yet somehow like a teen-aged girl playing at being a queen.

"Your hair looks lovely," I said. "I like it that way."

"It's functional," she said. "It's a kind of protection. It took me two hours to do, and I'm not very likely to let you mess it up."

She sat down on the couch and leaned back, as if she'd just finished a prolonged struggle and was exhausted. But she wore that trapeze-pin, and she was fingering it. She had it on a black dress this time, wool, with a row of black cloth buttons running diagonally from her right shoulder to the left side of her waist. There wasn't another break in the primness of the dress. And it was high necked; too high necked for the way I felt.

"Drink?" she asked. "All I have is brandy ..."

"Let's both have a big one."

I started to get up.

"Stay put. I'll get it."

That was the first chance I'd had to look around the living room. I don't know what I'd expected, but it was just another California apartment. Except that she'd done things with flowers around the room and a few accessories—modern figurines, ashtrays, and vases. Off in the corner there was that inevitable majolica-topped table that seems to be made expressly for California apartment house owners.

She came back and handed me my drink. She remained standing, holding her glass, near the small radio on the majolica-topped table.

"I like that dress, too," I said.

"How do you know?" she said. "You're looking right through it." There was an amused, tolerant expression on her face as she went on. "It's one of my bargains. After you take artificial flowers and excess doodads off a dress, and hitch it around a bit, it becomes an original Mona." She was going to say more, but she stopped because our eyes were fixed on each other. It was so quiet you could have heard a torch drop.

Then she half closed her eyes, and turned to switch on the radio.

"You look nice in that chair," she said. "As if you belonged there. I was thinking about it all day."

"What else were you thinking about?"

She didn't turn around, didn't speak.

"Where else do I belong?"

Now she turned around, and her face was a little sad. "That's something you'll have to answer," she answered gravely.

Answer that, if you can. Answer it. Go ahead, Thou shalt not covet thy neighbor's wife … That was the answer. That was the theme. That was something I had to shake out of my head, fast!

"What'd you do today?" I asked.

"I waited."

"What else?"

"I bought one of your books … The second one."

That warmed me in a different way. "Like it?"

"It's not a good book, but it's a fascinating yarn. You write too fast. You're too facile. But you can tell a story."

"That's what a writer should do. Tell a story."

She smiled then. "You had a line in there about how sexy it was when a woman put her lipstick on."

"It's true."

She nodded. "I never realized it before, but it is." She paused then. "How was I?"

"Fine."

The radio had warmed up and she raised the volume. It was dance music, slow and soft; not boogie. Together, with the same thought, we put our glasses down and met in the center of the room.

It was the first time I'd really touched her. My hand was on her back, at her slim waist. We didn't dance, we flowed like molten metal. But before I lost track of what I was doing, I snapped the lights out as I passed the switch. Only a standing lamp remained, near the couch, And dancing past that, I kicked at the wire, so it was out front where I could pull it out later with my foot.

The odor of Tigress drugged me, and the touch of her hair on my face, and the feel of her touching my body and moving away again. Touch, touch, touch. "Tigress, tigress, burning bright …" What was the other line? "And what shoulder, and what art, could twist the sinews of thy heart?"

She stopped suddenly and took her arms away from me. She went over to the radio and switched it off.

"Damn me, for being married," she said. "I could be just as happy with you without being so uneasy. Without feeling hesitant, and careful and a little bit ashamed myself."

"The little old man walks again ..."

She nodded.

I walked around restlessly and found myself at the hall. There was a door. I opened it.

"That's the kitchen," she said.

I looked in and walked on. Bathroom. Spotless. Clean towels. And then another door. The bedroom.

It was a double bed, low, with no footboard. Candle wick spread. Blue. I just glanced at it and then turned to look out the window. The rain drops hit the pane, grouped, and then ran swiftly down. I heard her behind me.

When I turned, she was at the dressing table. I moved toward her. She saw me coming up behind her. She opened a drawer and reached in, but her hand stopped. I looked down. Face down in the drawer was a leather picture frame. And I knew what it was. It was a picture of him. Not the kind they probably took of him at the jail house. No. A romantic one, a picture full of memories that chained her.

I didn't even touch her. I went back into the living room and sat down on the couch. When I heard her coming back, I moved to the other end of the couch, near the lamp cord.

She sat down, far away from me, but on the couch. All I could hear was the drip-drip of rain outside the doorstep. That and a pounding in my heart that got louder and louder. Then I put out my foot and placed it on the light cord. The edge of my sole found purchase. I moved my foot. The plug came out of the socket.

We were in the dark.

I didn't mean to say it, but I heard myself whispering, "Tigress, tigress, burning bright ..."

But I didn't get any further. I heard her move, and I turned to meet her.

It was a short, hard kiss, but the tip of her tongue flicked across mine and it was enough to cremate that little old man.

Then she pulled back, panting. I took a deep breath. I needed it.

"Maybe I'd better go," I said softly. Go? Me? Six strong men with rifles could make me do it. A team of stallions could drag me. But

I'd drop dead right outside the door.

Her voice was quick, uneven, metallic. "I had good intentions. I tried. Really. Tried desperately."

I leaned over and put my cheek against hers. That's when I felt her tears. And I felt bricked up, in a chimney; in a tomb; suffocating.

"Darling, don't cry. It isn't worth it. I don't want to hurt you. I don't want to feel tears on your face."

"You're a liar. It sounds good. But it's a lie. I know you don't *want* to hurt me. But if you have to, you will. I don't want to hurt you, either. But we're both going to get hurt." Her voice went lower and lower. It was almost a growl when she said, "And I don't care."

When I kissed her then, she leaned back. The feel of cloth and the touch of the row of buttons. Fumbling. Slow. She reached up and pulled. A button ripped off and rolled across the floor. The click of the button against the far wall was the last sound I heard for a while. Because the dress came down to her waist. She wore no brassiere.

Her shoes dropped off when I picked her up. I lurched against the hallway wall. Inside. Kicked the door shut. And the candlewick spread was rough. She pushed me away and got up. Outlined there, moving quickly, she tore her clothes off. I could hear her heavy breathing as she yanked the stockings. Her hair was down. She threw the covers back.

I sat on the edge of the bed, ripping my shoes off. My socks. Her fingers moved over my back, lightly, lightly … and the rain drummed, and my heart pounded, and then I was burning on the cool sheets. Close.

Tigress. Tigress.

"What the hammer? What the chain?
In what furnace was thy brain?
What the anvil? What dread grasp
Dare its deadly terrors clasp?"

Tigress. Tigress. Burn me bright.

There was a tunnel, running straight up, and I was shooting upward through it like an express train, up toward a pin point of light. Out of that dark tunnel, and exploding into a Roman candle flash in the sky. And then I opened my eyes, and I could see the room again.

"Merry Christmas," I said huskily. "Don't you think everybody should receive delayed Christmas gifts?"

"Darling," she whispered.

"I love Santa Claus, and unwrapping gifts, and tigresses, and especially you."

"Darling," she whispered.

"Mona ..."

She sighed. Her voice was tired and small. "You've messed my hair after all."

"I should think so," I said indignantly.

She snuggled closer.

"You know," I said, "Japanese women sleep with their necks on little wooden trestles so their hairdos won't be spoiled. I'll get you one."

"Don't bother. Your arm's much nicer."

I touched her eyebrows with my fingers, traced her cheek and lips. She kissed my fingers. She was smooth. She reminded me of that Rodin statue, "The Kiss"—a man and woman, kissing, and the woman as smooth as human hands could make the stone. But Mona was warm, too, and alive. And with my hand upon her, she began to stir, and I felt like Pygmalion.

"Little man quite dead?" I asked.

"No. He fainted. But now he's coming to."

"Little late, isn't he?"

She nodded, smiling ruefully. "Has remorse set in yet?" she asked.

"A little."

"Odd, isn't it?"

"No." Of course it wasn't odd. Afterward the brain is clearer and urgency is gone—other departments in the mind start functioning again. That's why whores always ask for their money in advance. Because then they have no trouble getting it. Afterward, they get it grudgingly and sometimes not at all. That's how remorse affects a man.

I got halfway out of bed, sitting on the edge.

"There's a dressing gown in that closet," she said.

Accustomed to the darkness, I made my way to it. Then I put my hand inside and touched suits ... his suits. My neighbor's wife.

"Don't bother with it," she said then. "There's no reason for modesty now, is there? I want to see you. And I want you to see me."

"It'll blind me," I said.

Her low laugh made me tingle.

When I got back into bed, I made her wait until I had a cigarette lit and was all set, comfortable, to watch her. Then I let her get up.

She was something to see, and feel with your eyes. She didn't pose or stop or turn around. She just walked—like an animal. "Wood sprite," I said. "Dryad."

"I'm not even dryad behind the ears," she said, and then her giggle filled the room. "Wasn't that awful?"

"I wouldn't put it in a script," I said.

"Would you put me in a script?"

"Like that?" I said. "The Hays office would crucify me."

It was nice waiting for her to came back, tantalizing myself, pretending she wasn't home, pretending she wouldn't be back, and still knowing that she'd be there in a few moments. Right beside me.

When she came back, she looked troubled.

"What're you thinking about?" I asked.

"Claire."

"Why?"

"Well, at dinner tonight. It was very strange. She started out being annoyed because I was late. I stayed in my bath for over an hour."

I pulled her close. "That's something else that's wonderful about you," I said. "You're so clean, darling. So clean and sweet, to kiss and touch, everywhere."

She took a deep breath. "As I was saying, she was annoyed. Then she noticed that I was acting strangely. She said I looked secretive and happy. She seemed to know. She felt it. And she was envious. I denied it, of course, but I'm sure there was a smug, confident look on my face. She said there was, anyway. And she was down on me for it. Are you?"

"Not yet."

There was a long pause. Then I started talking, telling her about this European friend of mine who always said there would never be a complete culture in America unless there was also a new sexual culture, a change in attitude from the worst residue of Puritanism. She said our sexual culture is to blame for our divorce rate, and our frustrated husbands and wives, our neurotics, our frigidities and infidelities. And she claimed we weren't fastidious enough. No European of any culture would think of going to bed with someone before bathing. Cleanliness or the lack of it was sometimes closely bound to inhibitions. And we wouldn't have a sexual culture until there was a bidet in every bathroom, so that women went to bed immaculately clean.

"I met the test?" she asked.

I nodded. "That's why I went to the steam baths before dinner."

She snorted then. "God damn it, we *are* pleased with ourselves, aren't we? Isn't there anything about me you don't like?"

"No."

"You'll find some things. I will, too. It's too early."

"Maybe," I said. "But I can't expect too much of a tigress, can I?"

"No. I'm a wolfess. I wolfed at you. Right from the beginning."

"All right, you're a wolfess."

"You'd better look out. 'Cause I'll huff and I'll puff, and I'll blow your hat off."

"I'm not wearing one."

"Does it matter?" She grinned at me again, but her face was tense and her body was taut. She moved against side.

Tigress. Tigress.

"In what distant deeps or skies
Burned the fire of thine eyes?
On what wings dare he aspire?
What the hand dare seize the fire?"

Tigress. Burn me bright.

CHAPTER 6

Driving home that night was an adventure. I was astride a comet, and down below me were a lot of poor human beings cluttering up Wilshire Boulevard. I made a left turn up a one-way galaxy and I knocked a traffic stanchion off the Milky Way.

But one part of my mind was clear, anyway. One little part that had become frighteningly active since I first heard about Mona. Now that part of my mind hummed, and I acted upon its humming.

Near Sunset Boulevard, I stopped the car. Chewing gum from the glove compartment. Then the Lavender Water. Cap off; break the cellophane top; a few drops. Fresh and clean. And no more fragrance of the Tigress.

But that wasn't all. In the space of a few blocks, the humming behind my ears continued like a dynamo. I wondered if Mona knew Bill was going purse snatching before he did it. But I didn't think so. Yet I knew so little about her. Before, that little was enough; now it wasn't. Where was she from? How had she lived before? What did she believe? What made her click? What made the two of us click?

I wanted to know what made us compatible, what made us meet and merge, what similarities in background and upbringing prepared us for this moment. What environmental patterns, what psychological bases built us toward this inevitable wandering from our normal lives. What made it happen?

We're made up of every word we've ever spoken; of every single thing seen by our eyes, recorded by our ears, registered by our brains from the moment of our birth. If, then, two people can become so close—what similar memories do they have? What deep-seated records of domestic scenes, of admonitions and rebellions, of young determinations lived into fact?

Oh, yes; there was more to her than I had learned tonight. More of the tigress. Even in Blake's poem there was more.

"When the stars threw down their spears,

And watered heaven with their tears,
Did he smile his work to see?
Did he who made the Lamb make thee?"

It didn't strike me until I arrived at home that ever since the beginning of this episode I hadn't been interested enough to ask Sue how she felt. She never complains, and it was hard to realize that she'd been in bed for almost four months. She joked about it, remained lively and pleasant, and maybe that's why a lot of people came to see her. She didn't present a visitor with the common depression of invalidism.

She was still awake, reading a magazine, and waiting for me. And I made the switch from Mona without half trying. Suddenly I was a husband again, asking about his child, listening to what she said and did and ate. And after a moment's hesitation, I said I'd take Ann to the zoo on Sunday. When you promise a child something, it's got to be done.

"What are you reading?" I asked as I got into bed. So easy it was; so effortless. I was a husband again. Chameleon. Husband. It was like pulling rabbits out of a hat. But I was the rabbit. Mona said so. Scared.

"It's one of those stories about a bitchy wife who gets her just deserts," Sue said.

"Let that be a lesson to you," I said.

"How's that again?" she demanded. "You're lucky. You've got me. I'm just a damned nuisance right now, lying in bed all the time. But I'm not a bitch."

I grinned at her. "You know why you're not? Because I'd bash your pretty head in."

"If I didn't have this large lump in my middle," she said, "I'd ask you to try it."

I walked over and bent down, and I wrestled a bit with her, tenderly. Then I tweaked her nose and she smiled up at me. That's all. But that's plenty.

And it was so easy. Because this was a separate compartment in my mind, untouched by what had happened earlier in the evening.

"Talked to the doctor lately?" I asked.

"Today. He says I can stop the Pranone and the opium things," she said.

"That's fine, Pup. Pretty soon you'll be a wife again," I said. "If it's another one like 'Little Doll,' we'll be lucky people."

"Little Doll" was Ann.

Sue giggled. "I was playing house with her today. I was her baby and she was the mother. I was sick. And she wanted me to turn over so she could take my temperature."

We laughed a moment, and we were close; the way we always were.

Believe me, you can look at her with different eyes, and it registers in another part of your mind. You can go along with it, without trying. It's natural to you, and it's right. A tigress can be clawing at your insides, and there's no sign of it.

"Let's get to bed now, Puppy," I said. "It's after three, and you'll be very tired tomorrow." I yawned. Tired. Tired and hollow in the bones.

That's the way it was. No diminution of warmth. No change. Everything the same. But I wished she was able to get up. I wanted to write a little note for her on the bathroom mirror. We always did that before. We wrote in soap. Just silly things. "I love yez, Pup!" And maybe a little heart with an arrow through it. Or a skull and crossbones with a message under it; "Guess who loves you?" Sometimes we'd write little love notes and leave them around the house—small pieces of paper stuck in books we liked, in drawers, in coat pockets.

It was a different thing entirely. Separate. Apart. What's so terrible about it? All right—I'm a transgressor, I'm despicable, I'm a heel. But there's worse than that in this town. There's a European couple; he's a director and she's an actress. They're married, and they still live together. But they go their separate ways, without question, even with mutual blessings. Then, every Sunday at breakfast, even with other people present, they discuss their activities of the past week—what men and women were involved; how good so-and-so was; what this one said and that one said.

Anyway, I didn't feel as low as that.

As a matter of fact, I had more trouble with Mac than I did with Sue. And I think I knew it would be that way.

He phoned me before I left for the studio next morning.

"Hello," he said. "Can I let her visit him now?"

The abruptness of it took my breath away. "Yes," I said finally.

"How was it? You sound pooped," he said quietly. Even for him, it was quiet. His voice was a little hoarse. He cleared his throat.

"I slept late."

"How was she?"

"I'll tell you when I see you."

"Today?"

"No. I've got a conference at the studio," I lied.

"How about tonight?"

"I'm busy. We've got people coming to dinner." That was true, anyway.

"What's the matter?" he asked. "Not getting hoggish, are you?"

"Not now, Mac. I can't talk now."

"Why not?"

"I just can't."

He waited a moment. "Somebody there with you?"

"Yes," I said. And I said it with such relief that it sounded true.

"Oh … Well, I'll talk to you. Take it easy," he said. "And have fun."

"Sure. Good-by, Mac."

It made my skin crawl. I felt dirty. But what could you expect of Mac? That's the way he was. Lots of men went through that police training without turning out the way Mac did. Maybe you couldn't even blame him. He told me once about the things men did to be promoted out of the vice squad. A certain number of arrests, of certain kinds. Like the time a couple of members of the vice squad bored holes in the roof of the men's room in a city park so they could post a Mexican boy up there to watch for homosexuals. Or the vice-squad men who used to lure young boys into committing acts for which they could be charged with a "288." "Lewd and Lascivious" in the cop's book. Mac told me about a psychiatrist who used to be called as a police expert in those cases. He got a fee, of course. But finally he became fed up with it. There was a case involving a twenty-two-year-old homosexual. The vice-squad man had been in a private car, plain clothes. He had picked up the boy, made advances and permitted an act.

For once in his career as a police expert, the psychiatrist tore loose and analyzed the problem. To his mind, he said, any man who induced such an act and permitted it was, whether he knew it or not, demonstrating definite homosexual tendencies himself.

It threw the court into an uproar, and the boy's case was dismissed. But the psychiatrist never got a call from the Police Department again.

Mac came up from the vice squad.

Before going to the studio that morning, I drove around a bit with the top down. The wind was fresh on my face, cleansing. It was a new day. I was a new man. And I had Mona.

Sitting in the car, I remembered things—last night. The curve of her arm, the soft under part; the young-girl breasts; the sylph-like figure going into the hall. And that soft laughter, and then the whimper that came into her voice. I was right about my observation when she was putting on her lipstick; it tallied; she brought her lips back that way at the climax, baring her teeth. It was nice, remembering.

Sure, I went to the studio. You know what I did there? I started writing a poem, something I hadn't done since I was twenty-five. Then it turned into a sonnet, or part of one. It was coming along nicely, but wasn't yet finished, when I remembered the musician I had once met in a New York bar.

He was a little, fat, puffy man, who looked like a koala bear, but he was quite a man, and he knew why.

"With sex," he said, "a man must be a virtuoso. He must play on a woman like on an instrument. He must press the proper buttons and hold them just so long, no longer. He must handle his notes, his rhythm, his tempo, *just so* … and then he must play toward the crescendo."

I remembered the way he spread his hands, as if to say, "That's all there is to it …" And I remembered what I said to him.

"Me," I said, "I play chopsticks."

I thought she'd like that. So I picked up the phone and told her about it.

When her low laugh came over the wire, I knew what had

happened. Because suddenly I was Rachmaninoff, I was Iturbi!

"You're better than chopsticks," she said then.

"With you, I improvise. I'm a composer!"

There was a pause. Her voice was very soft when she spoke again. "If you're musically inclined, why don't you come right over?"

The car burned rubber all the way.

CHAPTER 7

That Sunday, when I took Ann to the zoo, Mona was still in her separate compartment, and Sue was in another. But that day, a seepage began.

At the zoo, we were standing in front of the tiger's cage. Just a little thing like that. Just standing there and looking at a tiger lying in the shade.

What's wrong with that? I don't know. But all the way home, I wasn't listening to Ann prattle. I used to hang on every word, guiding her pronunciation, explaining the wrong ideas children get, joking with her, playing games.

Mona was on my mind, and she didn't belong there. This was Ann's territory. Husband and father territory. No trespassing.

That was a laugh, a deep laugh inside me. I was the trespasser, wasn't I? Trespassing against some kid, who laid his heart on the line for Mona, stole for her!

Well, that's when I first began to notice it. The little breaks in the compartment, the little intimations of a merging of my two separate lives.

Because habit had begun to creep into my life with Mona. First it was my Squibb's toothpaste. I bought some and took it to her apartment so I wouldn't have to use hers, which had a peculiar taste and a recognizable odor. Then it was the soap I bought, the same kind I used at home and the shaving cream and the bottle at Atkinson's that I put in Mona's medicine cabinet.

The rest was unchanged. The magic remained, as if Mona spoke a language nobody but I could understand. She was from another world. Nobody knew about her but I. She was my secret.

And I still didn't want to analyze the magic. We stayed away from talking about her, or Bill, or me. Both of us hedged on those topics. It was enough that we were together. And no matter how long I stayed with her, I always left her place crazy with wanting her.

But she wouldn't stay in her compartment anymore.

It must have been Tuesday when Mac phoned again. He'd been

patient; you had to grant him that. He'd waited. Tongue hanging out. He had control. I'd never have done it.

During those two days I hadn't seen her. We'd just talked on the phone. After all, I'd been back to see her on Sunday night, when I was supposed to be at a movie. I felt as if I'd been dry cleaned. But I kept wanting her, like an armless man reaching for something.

And all this time Mac was in the back of my mind like the rumble of far-off thunder.

Kate had orders to tell him I was out, in conference, away, unavailable, anything. There wasn't any Jon Forbes anymore. I was a new man. Forbes? Never heard of him. Gone. Sorry.

Then, like a fool, I absent-mindedly picked up the phone when it rang.

"Jon? Mac."

"Hi," I said, not at all cordially.

My office was on the second floor, but the ants came up from the studio garden anyway. There was one crawling across my script—the script that might just as well have been written in Sanskrit or in some language to which there was no Rosetta stone. I hadn't even thought about it.

"Where do I meet you?" he asked.

It was routine; police work. On schedule. Matter-of-fact. Turn her over like a check to a parcel at the railroad station.

"What about?" I stalled.

There was a long pause. "Oh, just to gab," he said then.

"I'm working like hell," I said.

"How's it going?"

"Fine."

"Seen Fred lately?"

"No." Fred? I hadn't seen anyone except the couple that had been to dinner the other night. And I scarcely remembered them now.

He paused again. It was such a simple trick. He would have continued it indefinitely. He'd never have hung up without an answer. He was just waiting for me to start spilling.

"Mac …"

"Yeah?"

"It's too quick. I … I can't. She's not the type you thought she was."

"Chinese?" he said politely. "Dead, maybe?"

I put my thumb down on the script and crushed the ant. "Mac, I'm not kidding."

"I know. Romance has set in. 'Hearts and Flowers.'" He started whistling it. "What are you giving me?"

"Nothing."

"Okay," he said then, "I know how to wait. But don't forget me."

"No."

"Code two. Remember?"

"Yeah. So long."

"Code two" was a police radio call. It meant "hurry."

I think maybe if I'd been out in my car and had seen Mac's police car on the road, I'd have crashed into it full speed and killed him.

Accidents happen, you know, even to cops. And it would have to be something like that; nothing else would stop him.

What did I do? Hold on to your hat. This ought to tell you how it was with me. Because right then I opened my desk, took out a couple of sheets of paper, and worked on the sonnet.

About a half hour later Brawley phoned and asked me to come to his office.

Walking down the hallway, I heard the typewriters going. Other writers were doing their work; most of them were happy about it. Their lives were somewhat circumscribed; they had families; they had impregnable routines. They were normal, as far as it's possible for writers to be so. But I pitied them. They didn't know Mona.

Neither did Brawley. That's why he could talk about the script as if it mattered. He had a suggestion for the last part of the story, he said; and if I approved of it, if it would work, maybe we ought to put it in the script.

Oh, he had a suggestion, all right; and it was good. But it was minor, and I knew he was merely trying to get me back into the working mood.

He kept me there for a long time, until after six. And all the time he spoke to me, he seemed to be examining me as if I were an unusual specimen of some sort. It made me uncomfortable.

What was I doing—calling one of the characters "Mona?" Had I started talking about her?

"What's the matter? You look uneasy about something. Don't you like it?"

"Yes. Very well." He looked at me quizzically. "Are you uneasy about anything?"

"No."

Then I promised to start working again.

There was a puzzled look on his face when he said good night. He smiled, but there wasn't a smile in his eyes.

I should have quit, I suppose. But I didn't want to leave him with half a script.

After all, I was only halfway through my story with Mona, and nothing on earth could have made me stop in the middle of that one.

It was after six, and the studio lot was almost empty. Kate never waited for me unless I asked her to, so I didn't stop at the office.

A little while later you could have snapped a picture of the typical American family right in my bedroom. A pregnant wife, a husband, and child playing on the floor. Happy music in the background, if you listened hard enough. Laughter in the house. A man at home. An advertisement for the Home Owners Loan Corporation.

Sure. That's what it was like. We were singing nursery songs, playing hide-and-seek, roughhousing. And the fat little Buddha stood on the bureau with just the right touch of sickening sentimentality.

At least that's the way I felt about him when the phone rang.

How did I know something was going to happen? Maybe I didn't. Lately, I jumped every time the phone rang at home.

It was Kate. She wondered if I had gone back to the office before going home. She left a message. A Mrs. Smiley phoned.

"Oh ... Right now? Does he want to see me now?"

Kate got it. She played along. "Yes."

"Oh, damn. All right. Thanks. See you tomorrow."

See how easy it was now? See how it kept popping into my mind? I hadn't had any intention of seeing Mona that evening.

Not until the phone rang, anyway.

Sue looked annoyed. "It's almost time for dinner," she said.

"I know ... I know ... I'll try to be back quickly. Maybe I will," I said.

So I kissed them both, like a husband and father going off to work—for them.

I got my coat and hat, opened the garage doors, and drove off whistling.

Just because I felt like it, I wanted to bring Mona a gift. Then the gift turned practical on me. I decided to go to Schwab's Drugstore and get a bottle of Chanel Number 5. That's what Sue used. If Mona began using it, too, there wouldn't be so much likelihood of my coming home with the fragrance of Tigress on me.

These past few days, the Tigress scent was everywhere. At the studio, in Brawley's office, on Kate when she went by my desk, and even on Ann.

The Schwab brothers can get anything, and I knew they'd have Chanel Number 5 even though no one else in town had had it for months.

It's a strange place, Schwab's, with an atmosphere peculiarly its own. It isn't large and it's far from attractive, but it has an air. It's movie-town's drugstore, and better stories are enacted at its counters and in the rear of the prescription counter than many a studio shapes into its best product.

The Schwabs know everything. The affairs, the quarrels, the loves and break-ups, the illnesses, the politics, the ups-and-downs. Everyone confides in them, from top stars to their servants. Once, when I had just gotten my first large sum for an original story, I walked dazedly into Schwab's right after I closed the deal at the studio. I walked up to the prescription counter, and Bernard Schwab was holding out his hand to congratulate me. He'd heard about it already.

Another time, Leon Schwab phoned me at the studio to tell me that my wife had just been to the doctor's office and that the rabbit test proved she was really pregnant, and everything was fine.

Once I caught Jack Schwab eyeing an emaciated, but attractive, blonde at the counter. I watched him walk over and talk to her a while. So I began to check with some other people about it. Just curious.

Then I found out that the Schwabs run a mission, too. They see the young girls flocking into town from all over the country. Some of them make good; others make good in another way. They start slipping into the hands of the wolves. But there are a few who keep fighting, stay away from the wolves, and never know when they're licked. They just don't want to go home. Pretty soon they're in Schwab's, having a cup of coffee for lunch, and nothing else. A bowl of soup for dinner. Literally starving.

That's when Jack or one of the others moves in. They've seen so many of these broken, bewildered kids. They take them into the back room and start talking, loosening them up. And if the girl can be convinced that it's no disgrace to return home without having become a star—the boys buy her a ticket to wherever she belongs, give her a few bucks extra, and see her off at the station.

That's Schwab's. Safe. Discreet. But I didn't want discretion. I wanted privacy.

So far, they couldn't know anything about Mona. She wasn't in the picture business, and she didn't trade there. But what about my charge account? How could I put another bottle of Chanel on the bill, especially since they knew Sue had bought two bottles only a few months before?

I waited around the magazines, paging through them, until the Schwabs were all in the back room. Then I got a bottle of Chanel from the clerk. I paid cash for it.

And I was on my way.

So I came bearing my gift, and with a sound in my heart like far-off music. I stopped at crossroads and let other drivers go ahead of me, acknowledging their grateful nods with a lofty wave of my hand. I loved everybody. But especially Mona. Especially the tigress, burning bright inside me.

And she wasn't there.

Maybe the tension and the exhaustion gets you in the nerves. Maybe the excitement breaks you down. But I was so disappointed, I could feel tears come to my eyes. Like a baby.

I don't know how long I stood there, ringing the bell, hoping she was inside somewhere, in the bathroom, maybe, not hearing. But then a passerby happened to look at me, and I felt foolish. I got back into the car to wait.

It's a long ride down from the crest of a wave like that. The early part of an evening is sad enough; alone, waiting, it began to get me. Night closed in very fast. Closed in deep inside me.

I turned the car radio on, but I didn't hear anything. Pretending she'd be home soon was a waste of time; I knew she wouldn't be. She was out with Claire, probably. Dinner. But I wasn't hungry. I wanted to be there when she got back. I wanted to see her coming up the sidewalk. I wanted to see her face light up and those gray eyes narrow as she smiled.

I waited.

Other doors opened and closed; other lights went on. Men and women came home. Everybody came home. She didn't.

It was after nine, and I began to walk up and down the street. Whenever I got too far away from her door, I'd hurry back, thinking she might have slipped by me.

Finally, I walked up to Wilshire Boulevard and went into a drugstore to phone Sue. I told her I'd had dinner at Brawley's, and we were going to work on the script. Don't wait for me, I said. I hung up quickly.

No; don't wait for me. I'm busy waiting for someone myself. I'm waiting with my heart hanging out. I'm waiting for someone with a bottle of Chanel Number 5 in my pocket; your perfume. No, not for Brawley. Brawley has become a tiger. A sleek tiger. Don't look now, but the tiger is turning into a tigress.

But she wasn't there when I got back. Now it was ten o'clock. And what could I do about it? I didn't even know where this Claire Garner lived. In fact, I didn't even know whether she was with Claire.

That's what began to drive me crazy. It had never entered my mind before. It had never dawned on me. Maybe Mac got in touch with her.

I never realized before that you can watch yourself boil over. One part of my mind remained detached, observing and recording the wave of heat that rose to my head, the boiling in my veins. It was like the sound of a train thundering past.

Sure, be calm, I said. Think about it. If he hadn't dared approach her before, he wouldn't dare do it now. Except: now that he knew I had her, why should he wait? But he couldn't phone her, cold, and make a date, could he? Of course not. Except: he would have done just that if he hadn't been the one who arrested her husband, if she hadn't ever seen him before. There were lots of exceptions in that thought process, and every one of them hit me heavy and hard, and right over the belt buckle.

I went through two packs of cigarettes, and then picked up the butts and smoked them, too. And I sweated and cursed and waited.

It was cold. It was cold down to the nerves in my body. Now the lights were going out in the other apartments and in the houses along the street. Fewer cars came by. People were going to sleep, resting for tomorrow, putting calm heads on their pillows, putting sleepy arms around someone. And I was sitting in my car hating a man so much that it made me want to throw up.

And all the time, every moment, I devised ways of killing him. I could jump him when he came back with her, and slug him with the flashlight I had in the car. I could wait until he came out, and then, if he parked on the far side of the street, I could run over him. I figured he'd come from Wilshire and park on the right, so I turned my car around, to be ready.

It was very satisfying, thinking I had the guts to do it.

But it never came to that.

At one-thirty I went home.

The moment I came through the door, I walked into the den, closed the door, and dialed her number. While I heard the buzzing on the wire, my hand was rubbing the smooth red leather of the armchair. Smooth as tiger skin. Smooth as the polished black belt Mac wore.

Every time the phone buzzed, I died a little.

She wasn't home.

CHAPTER 8

First thing in the morning, I phoned her. Without even dressing, I hurried downstairs. I couldn't wait.

This time she answered, and her voice was sleepy.

"Where were you last night?" I asked. I kept my voice low.

"At Claire's," she said. "That's what I phoned you about. She was lonesome so I had dinner with her and we just talked till about two. Why?"

"I was over," I said. "You weren't there. So I was worried." All I went through last night, and I said it so simply.

Her voice warmed. "Oh, darling …" she said. "I'm so sorry …" Then she brightened. "Can you make it tonight?"

"No. I … I've got an important dinner party. Business. You know, story I wrote. I have to discuss it with a man." We had four people coming to dinner; I couldn't ditch it. Two good friends were coming, and a couple we'd met at a party some months ago and had invited to our house for the first time. The husband decided he couldn't ditch it.

"Now?" she said. "Can you come now?"

"Well … I'd better put in an appearance at the studio. Then I'll get away," I said.

"I'll be waiting, darling. I won't even get up," she said. "You can make my orange juice and coffee for me …"

All the fear and anger flowed out of me, and I breathed once more because she was safe.

But I wasn't safe. I had a feeling I'd never be safe again.

At the studio I outsmarted myself by phoning Brawley's office. It was so early that I didn't think he'd be in, and I told the secretary to say I'd be in to speak to him sometime late in the afternoon. With that established, I figured he'd let me alone until then.

But he was in his office already, and he asked me to come over.

I had to phone Mona and call it off. But I promised to be over right after I finished my conference with Brawley. We were sure it wouldn't last long; certainly not later than twelve or one o'clock.

But it almost seemed as if Brawley knew my intentions and delayed me deliberately. We discussed the script and my attitude toward it; we discussed casting and budget, which are not my concern; and we talked interminably about people and stories and studio policy. Then, along toward one o'clock, he asked me to have lunch with him. He had some other story points to discuss.

You're helpless in a spot like that. Especially since the man seems interested in you personally. He asked me whether my personal problem had been solved, and he again offered his assistance. I told him everything was fine, but he looked skeptical.

He looked so skeptical that I began to worry about what he knew. It wasn't possible that he knew. He couldn't know.

But he kept me with him until nearly six o'clock. Then, because I knew I could still be home in time for dinner, I went to Mona's.

The smile on her face when I came through that doorway was something to remember, something to grow old with. When a woman has that look on her face, she's yours. Not just now; not just physically; but till the candle burns to the ground.

"I didn't think you were coming," she said.

And when she let me go and I caught my breath, I handed her the bottle of Chanel.

"I had it for you last night," I said.

"Don't mention that. It makes me miserable to think I wasn't here. But I didn't think you would be ..."

"I walked up and down outside like an adolescent mooning at his love."

"Darling ..." She stopped in the middle of opening the package. "Don't talk that way ..."

I grinned. "Don't get that tigress note in your voice. I've got to go out to that dinner. Besides, I'm so pooped, I'm not dangerous ... not even to you, lovely as you are."

The hoyden look came over her face. She opened the box. She didn't play out an emotional act; and she didn't treat the Chanel as if it were just a piece of gum. She liked it, she said so sincerely, and she carried it into the bedroom.

I waited in the living room. "Don't lure me in there," I said. "It's no use."

I could hear her moving around in the bedroom.

"I'm not luring you—though you lure easily," she called out. "I'm busy, too. I've got a dinner date with Claire, and I've got to take a bath."

A shoe hit the floor.

"I ought to get going," I said.

Another shoe dropped.

"What did you say?"

"Mind if I stay a while?" I said.

More sounds. Soft sounds. Bare feet on the floor. Then I started down the hall.

She was sitting before the dressing table, as white and smooth as marble, with that slim, almost androgynous, figure duplicated in the mirror. She was taking her black hair down.

I lounged in the doorway.

"I've got to hurry ..." She got up.

"You'll never make it," I said slowly.

"Oh, yes, I will. Make way," she said, laughing up at me, close now. "Move."

I let her pass. "Bitch," I said tenderly.

"You made me one," she called from the bathroom.

"That's hitting below the belt," I said.

"And perfect aim," she said mockingly.

The water was running into the tub now. I walked into the bathroom and stood near the door.

"Don't look now," she said. "I think my slip is showing."

I didn't answer. I should have been on my way home by now. I was late. I was tired. But I was waiting.

"This is a mean trick," I said morosely.

"I know ..." She stepped into the tub and sat down. "I never intended to do it. But ... you said you weren't dangerous ... and I ..." She looked down, like a mischievous child. She had the body of a child—or rather a mature child.

"You thought I couldn't resist ..."

She shrugged. "You can't," she said.

She was right. I was taking my coat off.

Almost two hours later she remembered to phone Claire and break the dinner date. But I didn't even think of phoning home.

"Jon ..."

"Mmmmmm?"

"I did this purposely."

"I know."

"No. I mean I didn't want you to keep that dinner date you had."

"Why?"

I could feel it coming—everything we'd skipped, everything we hadn't dared talk about for fear of breaking the spell. Now there's no way out of it. If this didn't shatter us ... nothing ever would.

She turned over on her stomach and leaned half over me, examining my face.

"You've got that scared look again," she said gravely.

I didn't answer. I waited. This was something I didn't want to start. Maybe it wouldn't start. Maybe we could get by it again.

"Where'd you get my name and phone number?" she said then.

The truth about that was heavier on my chest than she was. The answer was prepared, and it was going to be the only one.

She went on. "And don't tell me you saw my name on the mailbox. And my phone number isn't in the book. This has to be straight."

It was easier not looking into those gray eyes. It was better not to face them.

I told her I'd first seen her on the steps of the Beverly Hills City Hall. She was going inside, and I was behind her, visiting a friend of mine on the police force. It was Saturday, I said. My policeman friend found out who she was.

She drew in her breath. "Then you knew Bill was in jail. You knew I was alone. And you jumped me like a wolf."

It had to be straight. I made it as straight as I could. "Yes."

When I tried to go on, she put a hand over my mouth.

"I know," she said dubiously. "You didn't know it was going to be like this."

She was slipping away from me suddenly, and it was like seeing someone you love drowning, and knowing your mouth is taped up and your arms and legs are bound. There's nothing you can do but watch.

After a moment, she lay back, her head on my left arm, and reached for a cigarette. Lighting it with my right hand, I kept my left arm still so she wouldn't become aware of lying on it. I was afraid she'd ask me to take it away.

"All right, if you know that much, listen to the rest," she said bitterly. "He did it because we'd sold our car and were almost broke. He did it because he couldn't get a job and he didn't want me to work. He did it because he loves me." Her voice went cold. "That ought to make you proud of yourself! That ought to make you feel great!"

Why me, alone? What was she hitting me for? Sure I felt like a louse. What of it?

It poured out of her now. She came from Binghamton, New York, and had gone to Cornell, where her father was a professor. When she was sixteen, her mother died, and her father took to lushing. He lasted another year at Cornell before they kissed him off for habitual drunkenness. After that, Mona just packed up and went to New York City to become a photographer's model.

There was a small break in the story; she didn't say much about what happened in the small house in Binghamton where she lived with her father after he left Cornell. She just said it was horrible; and I gathered he was glad she moved out. She'd never heard from him since then, though she'd written about her engagement and her marriage.

She met Bill Smiley in an agency waiting room. They were waiting for a job, and they got it together. Posing for a Palm Beach kind of ad. In beach clothes. I gathered that Bill was something to see in swimming trunks, but I felt I could live without that experience.

She went on, telling me how lonely she was in New York. Her mother had been an orphan and her father had come over from France after the last war, so she had no other family. She and Bill got together because he was lonely, too. They were a couple of bewildered kids, and they needed each other, especially since they were just young enough to be appalled at the casual promiscuities they witnessed all around them.

Maybe it was the knowledge of those promiscuities that began their first troubles. Because right after they were married, Bill made her quit working. He wouldn't permit her to continue modeling. He was jealous. But she rather liked his being jealous; it was just a minor irritation then, and a proof of his love.

Then Bill began to do very well. Better jobs. His name beginning to be recognized. More money. And then a pressing need for a larger-sized hat. After an arrogant few months, he went downgrade very fast. But he was still cocky. He didn't have to model anymore. He could go out to Hollywood. He could act better than any of those poor hams he'd seen on the screen lately.

So they spent most of their savings on a car, and they came out to California with the Garners. And after a long time, after they had to sell their car, Mona wanted to go out and look for a job. Bill wouldn't let her. He'd take care of her!

A couple of days after they had their worst quarrel about her going back to work, Bill returned one night and announced that he was working in pictures. Just a bit part; but he was building it.

After that he went off to work regularly. Things were fine. And then a policeman knocked at the door one night and told her to come over to the Beverly Hills Police Station. Bill was in jail for purse snatching.

That was the gist of it. But it doesn't have the tones of voice, the things behind the voice. It doesn't have the catch in her throat. The emptiness isn't there. When someone you love speaks of being lonely, you want to do something. You want to offer your comfort—for all the hours of dusk and dawning that are the worst to spend alone, for all the secret heartbreak and the yearning.

She lit another cigarette, and I began to question her about her mother, about her girlhood, about everything I wanted to know. And it was all in pieces. Separate items I couldn't assemble into a clear picture.

Her maiden name was Duclos. She'd finished three years at Cornell. When she was a kid she was too skinny, and the stag line at dances never threw her a glance.

That's what I mean by little things that touched me. Because kids who are skinny, or buck toothed, or unable to measure up to the other kids around them in any way whatever, go through a torture few grown-ups could endure.

"I had that problem myself," I said. "When I was over twenty-eight, there was a day I'll never forget. It was the first time I ever stepped out on a beach that someone didn't call me 'Skinny.'"

"You're not skinny, darling. You're lean. You've got a beautiful body," she said comfortingly.

Then she waited, taking three or four puffs.

And I knew she was waiting for me to begin talking. But I couldn't. Because what she wanted to hear about me was not far enough back. She wanted to know about the present.

"This is true-confession hour," she said, finally. "You're at bat."

"I haven't a thing to say."

"Scared rabbit again?" she murmured. "Haven't you got the guts to be honest with me?"

Even though I'd been expecting it, it hit me hard. What do you say to her? How do you talk if everything you say is going to hurt her?

She didn't move. The cigarette was a little dot in the darkness that drew my eyes and held them.

"You damned scared rabbit!" she snapped, suddenly. She said it upward, as if she were speaking to the ceiling, and she still didn't move. She was rigid.

"Scared of the tigress," I said, trying to make my voice sound gay.

She went right on, venomously now. "Don't you think I've wondered why you never took me out? Don't you think I've wondered about your dinner parties?"

"What about them?"

"For one thing, before you arrived tonight, I'd already taken a bath. I took the second one because I wanted to keep you here!"

"Why?"

She shook her head in amazement. "Why? Why do you think?"

"I don't know." But I did. I did, but I didn't want to.

"You're married, aren't you?"

"Yes," I said finally. All right, I was married. So was she. What of it?

"So you finally said it," she said contemptuously. "You finally had the guts."

Sure I could have slugged her with the fact that she was

married, too. But she had never denied it. And I wouldn't have
hurt her, anyway; I couldn't hurt her.

"Any children?"

"Yes. One. Going to be four. A girl."

She was still for a moment, and slowly, deliberately, she turned
toward me. I thought she was going to kiss me. But she put her
weight on my chest, and then she jammed the lighted cigarette
against my shoulder.

I gasped, and began fighting her off. But my left arm was
pinned down. Her weight was on my chest. My right hand
couldn't reach over her. She held tight.

It hurt like hell. But I just relaxed my muscles and tried not to
feel the pain. Let it burn. Let it burn. It felt as if there were a hole
going right through to the bone. I bit my lip.

It made an acrid odor. My flesh burning. Mona was breathing
deeply, furiously, and her entire body was taut. At last she relaxed,
collapsing beside me, and in silence I could hear her tears
dropping to the pillow.

I should have been furious. But something else happened. The
viciousness of it excited me strangely. It brought me alive, like a
stiff shot of brandy.

But I didn't turn toward her. She was still lying on my left arm.
Still close. Still infinitely desirable. But the throbbing in my
shoulder began to distract me.

"That was for a lot of reasons," she said, crying. "It was because
I don't like your going from me to her or, for that matter, from her
to me. It humiliates me and it humiliates her. It was because
you're a lower bastard than I thought you were. You know why?
Because I have an idea your wife is someone I'd like! Because
there's something wrong inside me and I can't have a child. And
because you've made me feel cheap and low. I kept telling myself
I couldn't help this. And I couldn't! But, all along, I *knew* you were
married. I knew it! I knew it! I knew it!"

She was sobbing now. But I didn't dare touch her. It was better
to wait, better to let the anguish drain from her voice. That tone
hurt worse than my shoulder.

"I feel dirty!" she cried bitterly. "Don't you see why? My marriage
doesn't mean anything to me. It hasn't for over a year! But *yours*

means something to *you!* And don't lie to me! I know it does!"

She twisted and turned in desperation, as if trying to escape her thoughts.

"Darling, please … Don't torture yourself," I said gently.

"Why not? I deserve it! I'm half of this rotten mess. I knew why you brought that soap here. And god damn it, I know why you brought that Chanel here, too. She uses it, doesn't she? Doesn't she?"

When I didn't answer, she leaped up suddenly and sat on the edge of the bed.

"All right," she said. "Now go home to her with that burn on you. Let her see it. I only wish I had a hot poker so I could put a bigger brand on you!"

She yanked the candlewick spread off the bed and, wrapping it around herself, walked into the hallway. I could hear her gasping and sniffling. Then the refrigerator door slammed shut.

When she came back, she snapped on the light; but, even though it hurt my eyes, I peered quickly up at her. The way she felt, she might have come back carrying a knife. But instead she had in her hand a chunk of butter about the size of a golf ball. The candlewick spread trailed behind her as she approached the bed. Her hair was a mess, and her face was tear streaked, and her eyes were red. And she was beautiful.

"Lean over," she said.

I moved over on my right side, with my left shoulder up. A cigarette, held in one place, does a fine job on flesh.

She put the butter on and rubbed it around. It felt cool, but it didn't relieve the pain at all. She kneeled down beside the bed and kept spreading the butter. Finally I leaned back and she remained there, on her knees, enveloped in the spread like a Bedouin at prayer time.

"I'm not sorry I did it," she said then. "Maybe you don't understand what's happened to me? Maybe you think this isn't the first time it's happened?"

I just threw her a quick look, and she stopped.

"All right," she said. "At least you realized that. But let me tell you how I feel. Right after Bill was sentenced, I went job hunting. I found a job as a receptionist just a day or two before you phoned me. You know what I did the day after I met you? I phoned and told them I was sick and I couldn't take the job for a few weeks. They said they'd wait."

She wasn't looking at me now. Her head was bowed, and she held the spread tightly around her body, covering her all the way up to the chin, as if she were ashamed before me.

"I did it because I knew what was going to happen. I knew something had clicked, and I wanted to be right here at the phone if you really liked me and were going to call me. That's how it was."

"And how is it now?" I snapped it out, my heart pounding in rhythm with the pulse of pain in my shoulder.

"That's how it is now, too."

She still didn't raise her head. But when I put my hand out, close to her, she reached up and held onto it, tightly, tightly.

"I love you, Jon," she said solemnly. "I've got no morals anymore. I've got no pride. I want to be with you whenever you want to be with me. I'll take as much of your time and your thoughts and your love as you can give me. It'll be all I have."

Maybe that's when the burn stopped hurting, when her love seemed to take me in and smother me.

"I'll have to take that job next week," she said sadly. "I need the money. But it's only from nine to five … And I'll be home every night."

"Do you need any money now?" I said.

She didn't put on any spurious indignation. She wasn't insulted at all. She was straight, as usual.

"No. If I need any, I'll ask you," she said simply. She sighed. "The job will keep me busy while you're at the studio."

I took a deep breath. "What about when Bill gets out?"

She looked horrified. "Don't think about it! Don't talk about it! And don't ever mention it again!"

"It's odd," I said thoughtfully, "how indestructible those two little old men are … still picketing us."

She nodded. Then she reached over to my shoulder and spread the butter some more. It was running down my side. Her fingers on the burn made it hurt more, but it was a piercing pain that was almost pleasurable.

"Does it hurt much?" she said tenderly.

"Yes. But not from the burn."

"I know ... Inside. It's like having rocks in your stomach, isn't it?"

She put her head down on the edge of the bed, beside me, and slowly she began to cry again. Just softly, trying to release some of the despair. I know; because I wished I could cry it out of myself, too.

I couldn't. Tears might dissolve that hard sharp core of pain inside her. I'd carry mine around with me from now on.

CHAPTER 9

I had problems to face before going home that night. First: how was I going to explain my absence from that dinner party? Second: how was I going to explain that burn.

That burn required drastic action. I'd never be able to conceal it because I winced every time anything touched it.

Unfortunately, I was wearing my favorite suit, a light gray Shetland that I'd bought in New York. I hated to do it, but I couldn't take any chances. It had to be sacrificed to back up my story. A neat story. A dove-tailed story. One that answered both problems.

Here it was. After my long day with Brawley, I'd returned to the office to rest a few minutes. I'd fallen asleep. Sometime late at night, I'd awakened and dazedly lighted a cigarette. Then I'd fallen asleep again. The cigarette had burned right through my clothes. And that was when I'd first become aware of the time.

But to back up the story, I had to light a cigarette and let it burn through my jacket and my shirt. It had to be convincing.

And it was. It was so convincing that I sank much lower in my own estimation. Sue was waiting up for me. But before she could begin, I told my story. She didn't react to the burned coat and shirt. But when I peeled down, and she saw the burn on my flesh, everything but solicitude and tenderness went out of her. She told me where the Unguentine was and suggested I put some vinegar on first. She wanted to get up out of bed and help me.

I didn't let her get up, of course, but I think that's the only creditable thing I can remember having done that day.

That trust and that sympathy overwhelmed me. From then on, I was stunned. This house, and all the strengths that held it together, all the ties, memories, understanding, years of compromise and adjustment, years of love that had grown deeper with every month—this was what I had placed in jeopardy.

If you know how irritable and nagging some women can be when their plans are upset or they have been socially humiliated, you'll know how Sue should have acted. Her dinner spoiled; old friends in the house, and two new friends; but no husband. No husband and not even a phone call in explanation. Since she was forbidden to come downstairs, four people, our guests, had dined alone, as in a restaurant, before joining her upstairs to talk and drink and joke about my absence until it was time to leave and they pointedly refrained from mentioning me anymore. Oh, she told me how humiliated she was and how apologetic. But she told me now without bitterness and without anger. Because you can talk to her, and she will listen and understand. More than that, she will be reasonable. How many husbands can say as much?

Do you think I'd forgotten what I had? Do you think I'd forgotten for one moment my status as husband and father? No. I hadn't. That wasn't bothering me at all. But there was another thing. A small thing. An ominous development.

And that was the compartments in my mind. They weren't keeping Sue and Mona separate as they used to be.

There was a merging, and it frightened me.

It was a relief to have the atmosphere cleared with Mona, and it was a relief to know again how solid was the foundation of my life at home.

There was only one threat to my peace of mind. And that was Mac.

By now there was an edge to his voice when Kate spoke to him on the phone. He wouldn't be stalled any longer. I had to face him.

With a man like that, you can't trick it up. It had to be straight and it had to be good. That was my only hope. So I thought it out carefully. Even a cop had to have a heart. And I had to aim for it.

We arranged to meet at a bar on La Brea near Melrose on a Wednesday night. At about nine o'clock.

Maybe you think it was silly of me to be afraid of Mac. Maybe I thought so too, at that time. But you'll see what I mean. I was right. Mac was a cop, a good cop; but he was a bad guy. Just how bad he was is something nobody will ever believe. I can't prove it.

Anyway, when I walked in shortly before nine that night, he was at a booth near the door. He had an empty glass on the table. I sat down opposite him.

The waiter came over.

"How many have you had already?" I asked.

"Six," he said. "Why?"

I shook my head admiringly. At Fred's the night I met him, eons and eons ago, he'd gone right through a bottle, except for the one drink apiece Fred and I had.

"Another whiskey sour for the man," I said. "A bourbon and soda for me."

When the drinks came, we sat eyeing each other. In his civilian clothes, he looked even more massive. But he was damned good-looking. Powerful. Vital. With those alert brown eyes moving everywhere, even while he seemed to be concentrating on me. He had a dark gray suit on, a neat foulard tie, and his shirt was gray oxford. While I registered all this, he was watching me.

We drank silently for a while. He seemed to be savoring this meeting, waiting for me to begin. I let him wait.

It was a nice bar, and the people in it sounded nice, though I couldn't see most of them since they were in the other booths. But the few I saw looked nice; family people. It was a kind of family bar. Couples; groups; one family of mother, father, and two grown sons with their wives or girlfriends. The people seemed to know one another and the waiter. They were the kind of people who wouldn't be afraid of cops. You could tell that by their laughter.

A juke box played "I Couldn't Sleep a Wink Last Night"—a Sinatra number. Sweet, pleasing; but punctuated by the sound of a pinball machine near the bar.

Maybe he sensed our relationship had changed. I don't know. But to me, my antagonism was almost palpable. There'd been a kind of easiness before because I'd liked him; now it was gone.

"You took your time," he said finally. And he didn't mean with the drink.

"I couldn't help it, Mac. I was stalling you." That was the best approach.

"Why?"

It was excruciating to tell him about it, to strip myself bare before those cold cop's eyes.

There were some things I couldn't tell him; some things I couldn't ever speak to anyone; not even to Mona. But I told him how it was.

"Like being hit by a truck, Mac. Maybe you can remember how something hit you when you were a kid ... the first time ..."

"The first time was in a whorehouse," he said tonelessly.

It was like talking to bricks. It was digging into quicksand. But I had to keep going.

I can talk when I have to; my mind can write the words for my tongue; a typewriter taps away upstairs and the words come out of my mouth. It came out with romance at the edges. The inevitability of it was plain. The sweetness and the tenderness were enough to touch the heart of anybody but a cop—of *this* cop.

But I could see no reaction in his face. His eyes never left my face, even when he raised his glass. But I wasn't touching him.

"I'm in trouble with it, Mac. I'm off balance about it," I said earnestly. "I've got a problem. Don't you see that? If it were just a dame ... all right. But I don't know what to do."

"Let her go," he said quietly.

"I can't!"

"You just want your wife and her, too."

"Lay off, Mac. Please."

"This was my idea, boy. You don't want to double-cross me, do you?"

"Mac, I'm asking you as a friend—try to understand."

"No," he said. "It's your own fault. You let me build up to it. You let me think about it, too long."

"I did? You thought about it for a long time before you told me anything!"

"That was speculative," he said. "Maybe if you'd told me about it right away ..." He shook his head. "No. It would have been the same. It was thinking about you and her that really got me ..."

He had scarcely moved all this time. A solid bulk. No change of tone. No anger. Just flat statements.

"Mac," I said wearily. "I can't let you do it. Try to understand."

"I understand."

The suddenness of it surprised me.

"You do?"

"Sure."

Somehow, I wasn't convinced. I kept watching him. He was deliberate about pushing the empty glasses to the edge of the table. Then he wiped a wet spot with his paper napkin.

"Will you stay away?" I asked hopefully.

"No ..."

I leaned forward. My voice was threatening, I guess. I don't know now. "You'd better stay away, Mac."

And that was it. I didn't see him move, so I didn't try to duck. But my head bounced against the partition, and I faded out.

Vaguely, I could hear voices. Then Mac's voice.

"My friend's sick. Air'll do him good. I'll take him outside."

Then I was on my feet, and he was helping me down the wooden step. The bar was the front part of what must once have been a small family bungalow. There was a grass plot out front, and one around the side.

"Take it easy, pal," he said.

I thought he was sorry. He helped me when I stumbled. Then I began to think he must have hit me much harder than I realized. Because I kept bouncing around. One minute I could see the street lights, and the next minute they dimmed out on me.

Back and forth. Lights. No lights. Getting up, getting down.

"Help me up, Mac," I said.

"Sure." His voice was calm but still toneless.

That's when I realized what was happening. He was still hitting me. In the kidneys, and the stomach. Back of the neck. Shoulder muscles. Picking his spots.

For a minute I was proud of myself. He had the weight on me by about fifty pounds. But I was still standing up. Sucker; that's what I was. He didn't want to knock me down. He was taking me apart while I was still on my feet.

I tried swinging on him. It was silly. I don't even think I was able to clench my fists. But I was taking it. It wasn't hurting much, not yet. But it was growing.

Then it came over me. It hit me all at once, from every side, and in every part of my body. Except my face. He never hit my face. He was hitting me where it wouldn't show. Thoroughly the cop.

It came in waves, that mass of pain did. I was making hurt noises, too. They tore out of me, though I tried not to let him hear them.

"You'll never get her, Mac ..."

"I'll get her …"

He hit me again. Six of him hit me. Eight of him hit me. He was multiplying like rabbits.

"I'll kill you first, Mac. I'll find a way …" It must have gotten out of my mouth between gasps. He heard it.

"Don't be a cop-killer, boy. We don't like it."

Then he kicked me in the stomach.

The treatment was expert. I came to with my mind clear but my body a mass of hurt spots, each clamoring a complaint through my nerves. I drew up my legs.

Mac was still there. "Keep stretched out," he said. "You'll fold up like a jackknife."

When he came closer, I turned and got out of his way. He just pulled me back. He had a wet handkerchief in his hand. He bathed my face. Then, while I lay stretched out on the grass, he kneaded my stomach. He rubbed sore places. He gave me some relief.

After a while, I retched. Face against the grass. The grass was wet on my cheek. Cool. I tried to turn my face further down into it.

Then he dragged me over to the side of the house and I leaned against it, sitting up.

"Not a mark on you," he said.

I touched my jaw, hating him, hating his guts.

"Not a mark," he said with a lot of self-admiration in his voice.

"I couldn't control it, pal," he said gravely. "I just couldn't. After all, that was a dirty trick you pulled on me."

I didn't answer.

"Let's have no hard feelings," he said then. And matter-of-factly, "You'll be surprised how quickly the pain stops." He still looked neat. His tie wasn't even messed.

I started getting up. He just stood there, a large hulk looming over me.

"You still can't have her, Mac …"

"Okay, okay—just forget it."

"Will *you* forget it?"

"No. But I'll keep clear until you're through with her." He paused. "Have I got a deal?"

"You've got a deal," I said. He'd never live that long—he'd never live to see me through with Mona.

But he had ideas of his own about that.

CHAPTER 10

Mac had done a good professional job on me. I stayed home for two days, recuperating, with Marital Happiness beaming at me day and night with his brown teakwood face.

I told Sue I had stomach cramps, and she diagnosed it as an intestinal cold. She was right; cold as rocks. But she saw that I was taken care of, and she let me sleep most of the time. I needed it.

At least, I didn't have to worry about the phone anymore. Kate had told Brawley I was sick; so that was settled. I had settled with Mac myself; so he wouldn't soon phone. And I had no fears about Mona; she'd never think of doing it. Maybe she'd wonder what had happened to me, but she'd wait. I knew she'd always wait.

As a matter of fact, Ann was more disturbing than Sue. The first time she came in from school, at three in the afternoon, and found me in bed, she was puzzled. It was a startling occurrence in a child's world.

"Why is Daddy in bed all the time?" she asked, her voice going shrill at the end of the sentence. "Daddy shouldn't be in bed. That's not very nice."

"Daddy is sick, dear," Sue explained.

"Is he going to have a baby, too, Mommy?"

"No, dear," Sue said. "Only mothers have babies."

She lost interest in me, then. "When am I going to have a baby brother?"

"It will be a brother or sister, darling. And you'll have to wait. As I've told you, the baby isn't ready to be born yet."

"I want him now."

"He's too tiny to be born now. He's got to grow much bigger before he can be born."

"But I don't want him to be bigger. I want him to be tiny, so I can put him in my doll's bed."

"Well, we can't hurry those things, darling," Sue said.

Ann gave up, came over to me, and kissed me. "Don't be sick, Daddy. I love you all the time ..."

Sentimental; sure. Husband-father tripe. I admit it, but she was right. Daddy was sick in bed. Daddy was sick because he was in somebody else's bed, dear. Daddy was sick inside. Sick to his soul and his conscience and his self-respect. He wanted to throw them all up. But Daddy wasn't going to find it that easy, darling. Daddy was in lots of trouble. But he was having only a glimpse of it so far.

When I was up and around again, I felt rested. The pain was gone, except for the burn in my shoulder. But my confidence was restored. I felt safe. I was amazed at the facility of my deception. Successfully, juggling my two lives, I flattered myself that I was doing it deftly, maturely, and sensibly.

That spurious confidence lasted only a few days.

It grew from a couple of small things—a recognition of an action, a repetition of a sentence. From similarities of perfume, the soap brought to Mona's apartment, and a dozen other little things, it kept growing. The separate compartments in my mind weren't being preserved intact.

Mona kept moving in on Sue's domain.

First of all, she wanted to know me; that's the way of love. She wanted to know what I was doing at the studio, what I was thinking, what people I knew. And it was fun talking to her. She was alert, interested, and witty. Then I found myself telling her the same stories, the same studio gossip, the same script troubles and good scenes, the same anecdotes that I told Sue. I could have carried a transcript from home to her apartment.

But the worst thing was that she was interested in what went on at home. She wanted to know how Sue had felt about a certain scene in the script. She wanted to know what Ann had done and said that day.

Of course, with Ann, it was Mona's yearning. That was plain. But it went so deep, so intrusively deep.

It was interest. Curiosity. Love. It was a hunger to share more of my life. Odd things. Bits and scraps. It was a hopeless scavenging for parts of my life that weren't rightfully hers. She was crowding her way into my family.

And I couldn't stop it. Maybe that's how love makes you give of yourself, but every piece I gave, every intimate detail I revealed to her, left me with less of myself for my home.

One night, Mona touched upon another, imperative point.

"Doesn't she want you?" she asked in the darkness.

"Not now. At certain stages of pregnancy, there are flow points. She's not interested."

"That's quite a penalty to pay for having a child, isn't it?" she said thoughtfully. "But I'd pay it, too, if I could. For you."

So the small talk merged, and the colors and odors and touches mingled, becoming more and more like the pattern that meant home, the pattern that had been inviolably the property of Sue.

I felt she shouldn't have been encroaching that way, that she should have stayed out of there the way I stayed out of Bill's closet at the apartment. But there was no stopping her.

On our anniversary, Sue's and mine, it was only natural for Mona to mention that she'd seen just the gift that answered the purpose. I'd told her Sue wanted gold clips to match her watch. Mona said she'd seen a beautiful pair that could be joined into a lapel pin. At Trabert & Hoeffer's on Wilshire.

I went there reluctantly, because I wanted to choose my own gift for our anniversary. But I had to admit Mona was right. The clips were perfect.

So I bought them, and every time Sue wore them, there was a touch of Mona about them.

That's how the two of them began to blend, in a kind of emotional synthesis I was powerless to arrest. The process continued as the days passed, and its continuance became a known and orderly progression of events that were soon so familiar as to become less and less noticeable.

I think I always knew it couldn't go on indefinitely. But I didn't know how it would end. I refused to think of it.

Then, on Monday night, the real trouble started. Now, thinking back on it, I can recall that same sense of uneasiness, as if someone were staring at the back of my head or I could smell something burning. Like a fuse. Yes, a fuse that would keep burning, always a little faster, until it exploded.

That Monday night we were at the planetarium on Mt. Wilson.

What's wrong with that? We had to go places where I wouldn't run into any picture people. We went to lots of silly places— wherever we could be unobserved; wherever I could feel I wouldn't see anyone who knew me. Little movie theaters at the other side of Los Angeles. Restaurants whose only recommendation was that nobody I knew ate there. Lunchrooms way out in San Fernando Valley, beyond the Lion Farm. A deserted beach a few miles below Oxnard, where you could walk out and pick yourself a hollow in the sand dunes and lie there, safe, without ever seeing anyone.

The planetarium drew a crowd of plain people like us; couples wanting to be alone, groups of kids, a lot of old folks, and some serious amateur astronomers. Nobody looked at us.

Inside, we held hands like a couple of kids, and we came out a little bit awed by what we'd seen. At least, I was awed. Mona wasn't.

"No," she said. "It just helps me rationalize some things."

When she gets that grave look on her face, I know what she means. It wipes out the impudent wood sprite look.

"Us?" I asked.

She nodded.

We walked out to the railing, looking down on the city. The air was cool. I put my arm around her as we stood there.

"What about us?" I asked.

"Just that thinking in terms of stars and 'sidereal' time … it's comforting."

"How?"

"Well, it's corny, but convincing. That we'll be dead a long time … that we have only a few years … that we ought to be happy … that in a hundred or a thousand years nobody will know or care … that it's insignificant … that …" She paused. "That, well, that I love you."

"Don't reduce me to insignificance," I said. "It's humiliating."

"You know what I mean."

You know, after a time you begin to know a body so well that you can trace its every line and curve through the thicknesses of coat and dress. I could. Just standing there, savoring her with my mind's eye was thrilling. Not physically, I don't mean that. But the simple knowing that this woman beside me, this lovely, infinitely desirable woman, loved me. That was it. The warmth of it; the magic of it.

"I needed this," she said.

"Needed what?"

"Stars … time … perspective."

"Why? Worried?"

She sighed. "I visited Bill today."

"How was he?"

Bill. Bill who? Who was this phantom that kept appearing between us? I didn't even know what the guy looked like. A collar ad. A punk in a Beverly Hills jail cell. The owner of a closetful of clothes in the apartment of a woman I loved.

"He was fine except for one thing."

"What?"

"He was jealous."

It took a long time to digest that.

She turned sideways, half her face bathed in the glow from the myriad lights below us. Grave little face with those gray undine eyes.

"Listen," she said. "You have a habit of shying off disagreeable facts. Let's face this one."

"What's there to face?"

She sighed in exasperation.

"All right," I said. "He's jealous. He's locked up, and he wants out. He imagines things."

"Does he?"

"Well, doesn't he?" I demanded. "How could he *know* anything?"

"Don't you see that it doesn't matter whether he knows or not. He feels it. He suspects it!"

"What do you want to do about it?" I said quietly. Calmly. Oh, so calmly. The silent, controlled type. As if you couldn't have drained a bucket of ice water out of my heart.

"Nothing," she said. "But he'll be getting out soon."

Why didn't they keep him there? Why didn't they give him ten years, or life? Who the hell wanted him back? Mona?

"Is he coming back to *you?*"

"Yes."

Just like that. A mere nothing. Yes. Obviously. Home to the nest the mighty hunter comes—with a snatched purse in his hand. And the tigress, sleekly waiting; his mate.

It was like a smother in my throat. I couldn't talk anymore. I just took her arm after a while and piloted her back to the car. That planetarium and its god-dammed stars!

I wished we'd never come.

We drove down the mountain in silence. The little squeak in the clutch was loud and irritating. Every once in a while I glanced over at her, examining her grim face for some sign of weakening.

"You're a cruel, selfish bastard sometimes," she said finally.

"Oh, sure. That's what love does to you. A lean and hungry heart is a dangerous thing," I said. Then simply, "You think I care about him? Why should I?"

"How about me then?"

"You can leave him," I said.

Suddenly she moved closer to me and looked up, shaking her head adoringly. "I love you, darling. You're wonderful."

It made a singing in my heart when she looked at me that way. Evidently that's what she had wanted me to say. Then my elation petered out. I wondered if she expected me to say that I'd divorce Sue. But no; not Mona.

"Sometimes I adore you simply because you're so sweet and such a damned fool," she said.

It startled me. Her voice was a little cutting.

"Why?"

She shrugged and just nestled closer. Whenever I made a right turn, my arm would press against her breast, that lovely little-girl breast. I made four or five right turns before she noticed I was going round and round the block.

"Stop it, you idiot," she said, smiling. "Remember what you said. You're tired and you have to work tomorrow, and you're not even coming in."

"A man can change his mind."

"No, dear. Please. I know how you feel. I want you to come in, too. But don't forget you've got to work. As soon as I start interfering with your work, you'll begin to hate me a little ..."

"Okay. Okay."

She looked up again. "You know where I went yesterday?"

"Where?"

"To the playground at La Cienega."

"What for?" As if I didn't know, as if I hadn't seen her there, behind the Sunday afternoon crowd.

"I was just watching you with Ann—the way you discussed things with her. What ride to take next, and how many times; and whether to buy a blue balloon or a red one ..."

There it was again; that loneliness in her voice. And something else, too. Something that had been in her voice a little earlier.

"Why am I trying to fool myself?" she said suddenly. "I know what I'm going to say ..."

"Then say it."

"All right, here goes. You mentioned my leaving Bill. That's out."

"Why?"

"Because if I broke away from him, you'd be obligated to me," she said simply. "Someday, when you had one of those inevitable quarrels with your wife, when she suspected you or something, you'd find it very easy to come to me. And I'd be waiting for you, too."

"Isn't that good?"

"No," she snapped. "Because if I let you in, you'd hate me all your life—for taking you away from Ann, and from the life you've built up with Sue. Do you think I don't know that? Do you think I ever dreamed for one single moment that I had a chance of achieving that?"

The traffic was suddenly too much for me. Red lights flashed in my face. People cut in on me. Pedestrians wanted to throw themselves under the wheels.

"Well, to tell the truth," she said, then, in another tone, "maybe I did dream about it. But I'm not dreaming now."

"Neither am I," I said,

"Damn you," she said. "I always have to speak everything out for you, don't I?"

I was right in front of her apartment house now. The car was stopped, but I still didn't take my hands off the wheel.

She went on. "I've always got to cut my heart up for you—to make you see what you're doing to me. Just to prove to you how much I love you. But, even so, when Bill gets out, he'll need me. He isn't too bright, and he isn't much in any way—but he hasn't got anybody else. The way I was for so long. Alone. All alone. Every godforsaken night. Every godforsaken minute of the day."

She got out of the car.

"Wait a minute," I said slowly. "Don't go yet."

"No. Stay there," she said. She went around to my side of the car and leaned in. She gave me a hard quick kiss.

"That's why, after he gets out, I'll stay with him," she said.

She still stood there, stricken and small and appealing. "Now get out of here, you bastard," she said venomously. Then her voice broke, and there was a crying in it. "But ... God help you, you'd better phone me tomorrow!"

CHAPTER 11

I phoned her. I phoned her constantly. Because I couldn't see her during the day anymore. She began to work for Gloria Bristol, the town's top beautician, and she was there from nine to five.

That gave me time to work. Not that I did very much. Oh, the script was moving, but slowly, and I couldn't face Brawley until I had a lot more for him to read. I kept making apologies and promises.

But how could I work? How could I do it, knowing, as I did now, that when her husband was released we were through? I knew she meant it. Sometimes women resort to that threat when they feel the first waning of a man's interest. But that wasn't Mona's way. And there was no reason for it.

You know one of the reasons I wasn't doing much work on the script? I was working on that sonnet again. I finished it. It wasn't bad at all. I had it all ready for her now.

And that was the day that trouble began to move in faster. The fuse was burning faster toward the explosion. And the fuse had Mac's name on it.

She phoned me shortly after lunch. She'd just come back from visiting at the jail.

"This time, there's something definite," she said. "Someone's been talking to him. There's a policeman up there who's been making cracks about how pretty I am … and I shouldn't be allowed to run around loose. And it's driving Bill crazy."

I kept my voice steady. "Did you talk to him?"

"The policeman? No. Why?"

"Do you know his name?"

"No. But he's been telling Bill that he saw me in a car with someone … And Bill's raving."

"Okay," I said. "Don't worry about it. I'll have it stopped."

She was dumfounded. "You'll have it stopped? How?"

"I've got a friend up there, haven't I? I'll tell him to see that his pals lay off. "

"Well, all right," she said dubiously. "But … Jon, he sounded so sure this time. I felt as if he knew something."

"How could he, darling? Don't worry about it. Please. Leave it to me," I said.

"Jon, he'll only get angry with me. But he may make things unpleasant for you."

"He doesn't know anything about me." I hoped he didn't. I prayed he didn't. But I wasn't too certain.

"Will I see you tonight?"

"Yes. And I've got something for you."

"What?"

"Oh, just a little surprise."

"Tell me."

"No."

"All right. I won't like it. It's probably something useful—like a bath mat or a set of hair curlers."

"See you tonight," I said. "Don't forget me."

I hung up.

Maybe I thought I wasn't scared. Maybe I was so chilled inside that the emotion didn't register. But I didn't care if I had to take another shellacking. I had to see Mac.

I couldn't figure out what he was trying to do except make trouble for us. It wouldn't help him any. I knew that. But maybe he didn't know it.

So I had to make sure he knew it. Right now. Face to face. I didn't care if I had to run over somebody on his beat. I had to find him.

With all that tension building up in me from the time I drove out of the studio, it was a shock to find him so quickly. You'd think he'd been waiting for me. And maybe he was.

The moment he saw me wave at him, he pulled over and parked. He looked friendly, too, and it almost seemed as if we'd never had any unpleasantness between us.

He shook my hand silently as I got into the car.

"Hi, boy. Glad to see you."

"Same here, Mac. As a matter of fact, I was looking for you."

"Yeah. I thought you would."

"Why?"

"Oh, because of that gag I've been pulling at the jail," he said. "I made a crack one time, and he ribs nicely. So I kept it up. Today, one of the boys told me he'd been quarreling with Mrs. Smiley about it." He beat me to the punch.

The simplicity of it left me speechless. I was without a cause for anger. I was empty. And I felt foolish.

"But, hell, Mac, you're ribbing him and cutting my throat," I said.

"I know," he said. And he looked sheepish and apologetic. It was the first time I'd ever seen that big hulk looking that way.

"If it's just a gag, Mac …"

"Sure it is." His voice softened. "I told you I'd keep away until you were through, didn't I? I meant it."

"Okay, then, I just wanted to be sure."

"I'll cut it out," he said.

With all I knew about him, with all that had happened, how could I feel so reassured? Maybe it's the look he has about him—big, comforting, solid. The calmness of him, the strength of the guy. Sure, he'd been baiting Smiley, tossing darts at him as he would at a target. But I felt sure there'd been nothing deliberate about it. Malicious, maybe. Just a bit. The outlet for a man who'd been cheated out of a woman. That's the way he was bound to feel.

Then he began to ask how Mona was—and he kept probing, trying to obtain a vicarious pleasure from my words. He kept wetting his lips. And he was pretty open about his envy. He admitted it, but he wished me luck. And he also said he hoped one of us broke it up soon so he could move in.

"You won't live that long," I said. But grinning; not in anger. I kind of liked him again.

"I keep hoping," he said.

Then he wanted to gab some more, but I cut it short. The thing was settled. And now I had to go shopping for Mona.

You know what I bought? A bath mat and a set of hair curlers. She suggested them and she was going to get them. With the sonnet. It made a nice combination. It was silly, but right. Because I was a little worried about walking in and handing her the sonnet.

Oh, we'd read poetry together, and I was always bringing her books I thought she'd like—because they were the ones I liked. Graham Greene. *Alice in Wonderland.* Some other books I'd brought to Sue's attention, too.

But I was pretty far removed from my poetry-writing days, and, well, I just felt a little uneasy.

And it was the only thing I felt uneasy about. The Mac problem was settled in my mind.

So I walked in with my three gifts, put the two packages on the table, and sat down. She was pretty worried about Bill, and she was relieved to find out it had all been a rib at the jail. Then she opened the packages.

She had a neat little boyish suit on, gray and wide shouldered. When she began to laugh, she leaned over so her black hair, down now, came over one eye.

Laughter like hers can make your heart swell up inside you until you can't breathe. She starts giggling, and then lets it rise up and dance around the walls. And that impish look comes over her face—crinkling her little nose, crinkling around the eyes.

The little gag was well worth it.

Then she got to the sonnet. I held it out to her, and then wanted to walk out of the room. But there was no place to go, no place to hide. I just waited.

The laugh lines disappeared. Her face relaxed. And she began to read it aloud.

"I find no beauty in the classic face
Or in the body chiseled out of stone
In studied lines. I think the frozen grace
Of Grecian art was meant for sight alone.
But eyes see not—from beauty quite apart—
Another kind of beauty, like your own,
Which must be touched, and felt with tongue of heart
And lips of brain, to be completely known;
Which must be held as in a miser's mind
And fondled with the senses. Eyes have grown
So used to vision that they cannot find
What runs like wildfire underneath the bone.

But I have found that deep within you lies
A beauty I can know without my eyes."

Her voice faded to a whisper as she finished. Then I could hear her walk over to me. My head was bent over and I was looking at the floor, afraid to raise my head. But she was close now, and I rested my head against her and slowly put my arms around her waist.

Her hand came down and touched my head, gently, lightly.

"It was a dirty trick to give me that, darling," she said huskily.

"Why? Don't you like it?"

"You know I do."

"It isn't very good, but it's something I wanted you to know. I felt you were forgetting how much I love you." It was hard to express. "It's something I haven't done since I was a kid ..."

She didn't move. Her voice was far off. "You know what this does, dear? Do you know?"

"What?"

"It sinks us, darling. It means we're going to go on together after Bill gets back."

My hands tightened around her waist. That's what I wanted. That's what I'd been praying for. But her voice was cutting through my elation.

"It means we'll get to be lower and lower, until we're caught and trapped. And then maybe we'll turn on each other like the rats we are."

"Darling, don't say that." The cloth of her dress was against my cheek. Her warmth came through it. The warmth of the tigress.

"All right, I won't say it," she said softly. "I'll tell you only what you want to hear."

Then her voice sounded sad and far more mature, with a kind of old-crone wisdom in it. "I'll love you as long as I live, dear. Despite the fact I've become the kind of woman I've always despised, I'll never stop loving you. I don't want to stop. I can't help it. You and I have changed since we met. We're no longer as nice as we were. We're closer to animals ..."

"I don't care," I said hoarsely.

"Neither do I," she said. Then she sighed and pressed my head against her.

"Tigress ... tigress ..."

"Yes, I'm a tigress," she said shakily. "And you'd better carry me inside or I'll claw you right here."

So the fuse took another spurt and burned closer to the explosive. And me? I didn't know it; I was just glad everything was settled and running smoothly.

CHAPTER 12

Everything was fine.

At least, it was fine until I looked into my desk at the office and realized Smiley was coming home. We'd had a sort of housecleaning at Mona's, and I had to hide the evidence in my lower left drawer. The toothbrush, lavender water, soap, the whole stack of books, a couple of pieces of costume jewelry I'd bought at Adrian's, and the bottle of Chanel. It was like the debris of a calamity that hadn't yet happened, but was in the making.

Still we'd made preparations—phone call signals, for instance. If her phone rang twice within five minutes and nobody was on the line, she was to step out and call me. Things like that. Cunning tricks: Little subterfuges. Carefully planned.

But calm nerves couldn't be planned. The day he was due to be released, I was so wrought up it seemed to me I could hear my pulse beating.

I could tell I was far from calm because Kate was unusually solicitous. She walked around on tiptoe. She shut the door with infinite care as if the noise of its closing would jar my head off.

You know what got me? Not fear, but jealousy. The thought of his coming home to her was throttling me. The thought of his touching her, of the clean whiteness of her lying beside him, white and immaculate as a peeled sapling.

That night, Sue woke me up.

"What's the matter, Jon?" she said.

"What? Why?"

"You were gnashing your teeth. It woke me up."

"Bad dream," I said sleepily. "All a bad dream."

But whatever it was that I dreamed, the clutch of its nighttime terror stayed with me during my waking hours, through the waiting and the not knowing.

Two days went by, and then when I phoned Gloria Bristol's they said she hadn't been to work for two days. No news. No phone call. Nothing. She was at home, with him. She'd been there ever since he was released. And I sat at my desk, with the script before me, constantly examining the objects in the desk drawer because they brought her closer to me.

Waiting like that is a slow dying. Time passes, and nothing happens, but you slide closer to the grave.

The debris in the desk drawer now looked like souvenirs, the pitiful residue of an old love. Except that I couldn't let it grow old. It was fresh and burning, and would be so forever and forever.

Kate came into the office and stood near the desk until I looked up.

"It's none of my business, I suppose," she said, "but Brawley's secretary has been phoning me a lot lately."

"Why?" I asked absently.

"She wants to know how you're doing on the script. And whether you're in the office, working."

"What have you told her?"

"Not enough to put in her eye."

"Thanks."

She started out, then stopped at the door. She looked efficient and sympathetic, as if she were waiting for me to ask her for help. But I couldn't even talk to her. I just shook my head. She walked out again.

I didn't care about Brawley or scripts. I just wanted to hear from Mona before I went home.

I didn't hear anything from her. But still I didn't go home.

Knowing Smiley had never seen me, I took my chances. I drove by the apartment. Me, outside; Smiley inside, with her. The lights were on, but the Venetian blinds concealed everything. There wasn't even the movement of a shadow behind them. I know. Because I stayed there for a solid hour, watching, with my car parked right across the street.

It seemed to me that every passerby and every neighbor must have known me by now, must have known that I belonged in that apartment across the street. I belonged in there, and he didn't.

Right now, I belonged in there more than I belonged at home.

But I had to go home, finally. I had to go home and go through my own front door like a stranger. I was someone who just walked in to use the phone. That's where I went as soon as I took my coat off.

We had a signal. Two rings within five minutes, and then she was to call me back. But if I used it, she'd call me back at the office.

You know what I did? I knew she couldn't talk to me while he was there, but I just wanted to hear her voice. And I was lucky. He didn't answer it.

I heard her voice, her lovely warm voice. "Hello? Hello?" And then she hung up.

But even in that short space of time—time that stretched through all the days I'd known her—I knew something was wrong.

She was crying.

Do you know what that did to me? It was just as if she'd put out that cigarette on my naked heart.

But that wasn't all. Oh, no. That wasn't all I went through that night. That was just the early part of the evening. Just a curtain raiser.

Sue had that day been advised by the doctor that she could get out of bed. She could come down to dinner for the first time in months. She'd been waiting anxiously for me to carry her down the stairs because she still wasn't allowed to walk down. She wore a lovely black gown sent over from the Anticipation Shop, a gown that concealed all evidences of maternity. Her hair was done up the way I liked it, round and full to frame her face. And she was wearing the gold clips I had bought her for our anniversary— the clips Mona had chosen for her.

Then when I picked her up to carry her down the stairs, I was enveloped in Chanel—and the Chanel wasn't hers anymore. It was Mona's.

But I not only endured that; I went right down the line with every deceit in the book. By now it was natural. I didn't want Sue to know. I didn't want her to be hurt. Because I loved her. I knew I did. I'd never stopped loving her for a single moment.

As I looked across the table at her, the candles fuzzed my vision, and it was as if this were months ago, before Mona came along. We were, as before, indissoluble, and I was a husband who had never made a misstep. Because, until Mona, I had never wanted to.

"It's so nice to have dinner with you again, Puppy," she said.

Keeping my eyes off the clips was a constant effort. "I couldn't have picked a nicer couple of dinner companions," I said. "Shall we set an extra place for your little stranger?"

"No. His table manners aren't good enough. He's probably upside down right now," she said, laughing.

"That's my child," I said, grinning. "Bottoms up."

We drank water for the toast. "Here's to him—or to her."

She put the glass down then. "I had quite a time with Ann about that today. I was trying to prepare her for her brother or sister, letting her share in it."

I nodded. "I kept telling her she's just as responsible as we are, and we've all got to take care of the baby. She likes the idea."

"She likes it too much," Sue said. "I told her that we'd have to be gentle with the baby because he was so little. And she looked at me with great glee and said, 'If he's very very little, then we can hit him, can't we?'"

"Oh, fine," I said. "I saw her hit one of her dolls with a stick."

"Oh, don't worry about that. She'll love him. And she's very well adjusted to his arriving. She's waiting impatiently."

"Who isn't?" I said.

So we talked as we always did, and her warmth and affection were like an acid bath. I lied in my teeth and got away with it. I played husband and I got away with it. But, inside of me, I was sick. I was sick with deceit and with the horror of what I was capable of doing and saying.

I think I knew right then that it couldn't go on. The fuse was burning furiously toward the end. Nothing I could do would stop it; and now I didn't want it to stop. This couldn't go on, this mustn't go on.

But still I had to fake its continuance.

Upstairs that night, Sue thanked me for being so patient and thoughtful with her, for never becoming irritable with her, for bringing her books to read, and candy, and magazines, and occasional little gifts. I had been patient and thoughtful because my attention was focused on Mona. I had brought books that were duplicates of the ones I bought for Mona. And all the other little things had been bought at the same time as Mona's.

And the little Buddha on the bureau listened to me, and his fixed smile looked ghastly.

"I know it's been difficult, darling," she said. "I've been such a nuisance, and you've had to eat alone and do things alone. I know how much you dislike that … and I've missed you terribly, too. But I'll make it up to you when this is over and I'm not so awful and clumsy looking … We'll have fun together again. I'll make you dance with me until you cry for mercy … I'll wear clothes that will drive you crazy … And I'll let you rip them off whenever you want to …"

That's what I had to face. I never knew I could be that much of a heel—but the seed of it must have been in me, the seed of destruction.

That's what I had to listen to. That's what I had to respond to. Sue's love—that came down the years like an engulfing tide. Memories. Long-ago laughter and quarrels. Private jokes. The great strength of her that sustained me always. The faith that kept me afloat. All those things and more.

But now they struck from all sides with silent blows, the way Mac had beaten me that night outside the bar. Blows that left no mark, but were more agonizingly painful.

That was a night when the sleep mask and the ear stopples didn't help me. No sleep would come. Nothing could still the sound of Sue's voice. Not even Mona's, which spoke along with it. Not even the sound of thunder that I heard, thunder that wasn't there when I removed my ear stopples and raised myself on one arm.

No sleep. No peace. Ever.

CHAPTER 13

Sleepless and weary, I could hardly drag myself out of bed the next morning. My eyes kept closing even while I was shaving. Breakfast didn't do me any good; riding to the studio with the top down didn't do me any good. I was weighted down with vague fears that were growing and filling up the hollow inside me.

Most of the morning I just sat in the office, staring out the window with my brain numb and my fingers drumming on the desk top. Everything took on the bilious color of the sound stage across the way.

Trying to work was just senseless. I even tried popping a couple of "bennies" into my mouth, the way I'd been doing pretty regularly for a week or more. But I found I needed more of them. I suppose I was just enervated. I'd lost a lot of weight, too.

That's the way I was, loaded with Benzedrine and still groggy with fatigue, when Mona phoned.

"Jon," she said. "Darling ... listen ..."

"Mona. What happened? I ..."

"I know. It was you last night. Don't do that anymore, darling. Please ... I'm nearly going crazy as it is."

"What is it? What's the matter?"

"I don't know, but somehow he suspects. It's almost as if he knows." Her voice was low, but fast, breathless, with a touch of fear in it.

But hearing her voice was like hearing Gabriel's trumpet. I began to live again. The sense of the words she spoke didn't register. Only the sound of her voice was there, and it was like adrenalin, quickening the heartbeat and the pulse.

"He can't know, Mona," I said. "Unless you make a slip ..."

"I won't. Don't worry. But ... oh, darling, darling, darling ..."

"Mona, I ..."

The phone was dead. Just like that. She was gone. For a second I tried to pretend that she had hung up because she thought I was finished speaking. But it didn't work. I knew she'd had to hang up. Quickly. And I knew why.

He'd come back, and either he was listening or he was about to listen.

But which was it? Which was it? Did he know anything or didn't he?

But when you sit there telling yourself to think, telling yourself to do something, urging yourself into action—that's just when you draw a blank. Everything flows out of you. You can take Benzedrines by the handful, but they don't work. You can go to the window and try to drink in all the air in the world—but it won't let that black fog out of your mind.

I had to wait it out, sweating, bleeding in the brain. Nothing helped me. And I tried. God, how I tried. Within the space of three hours, and without stopping for lunch, I wrote forty pages of script. But they were so bad I didn't even read them over. I just dropped them into the wastepaper basket when Kate finished typing them that night.

Then I went home and worked in the basement at my workbench, repairing all Ann's toys that I'd neglected for so long. A rocking chair, and a little ironing board. A porcelain figure of a goose girl had to be cemented. The hair had come off a Raggedy Ann doll. I straightened up the nails and tools. I painted Ann's tricycle.

But it didn't help me. I had the fragrance of Chanel in my nostrils and I didn't know whether it belonged to Sue or Mona. I had a fear in my heart, and I didn't know whether I was more concerned for Sue or Mona. I was splitting apart. The whole top of my head was splitting apart. Somebody kept hammering a wedge right into my skull.

Now, I couldn't eat anymore. I began to live on orange juice and coffee, and a forlorn hope that somebody or something would step in and save me. Marines. Cavalry. Miracles. Voodoo. I would have burned joss sticks, if they would have given me hope. And I began to understand how all those faith traps and religious rookeries flourished around town. Men like me needed them.

You'd think there was magic in the "bennies," the way I was gulping them. In threes and fours ... because they wore off so quickly.

Another day passed, and then, the following morning, Kate came in and said Brawley wanted to see me. "What for?" I demanded. "Hell, I can't talk to him now. Not now!" I yelled at her.

"What shall I tell him?" she said quietly.

"Tell him I died. Tell him anything," I said. Sure, I'm dead. I'm burning, but not as brightly as before, not the way it was with Mona. This is brimstone.

I started getting up because Kate hadn't moved. She was just waiting.

"All right," I said. "I'll go over. I don't care if he throws me out."

"He'll have to," Kate said. "You'll probably collapse on his rug. Are you sick?"

"Yeah," I said vaguely. Very sick. A goner. Ready for that mortuary on Sunset Boulevard, the one with the clock and pendulum on the front of the building—a clock with no hands. Just a pendulum swinging a timeless warning of the end.

So I popped a few more "bennies" into my mouth and swallowed them quickly. They work fast. They'd keep me going during the conference with Brawley. But I realized I'd been downing far too many lately. They were bad for the nerves, but I had to keep going, didn't I?

Anyway, they hopped me up for the conference. They really did.

There isn't much I remember now about that meeting with Brawley. Except that he sat there behind his desk, his eyes on me all the time, following me as I paced the floor and talked. How do I know what I said? It was a full two hours, I think. Pacing and talking. Script and story, at first; then me; then the characters in the story; then me; then me and me and me. And all the while his eyes looked friendly and pitying and worried.

I didn't even stop when his phone rang. But then he handed it to me.

It was Kate.

"I didn't want to bother you while you were with Brawley," she said. "But Mrs. Smiley phoned three times. She wants you to come back here to your office and wait for her to call again. She says it's urgent."

The numbness came again. I just put down the phone. No good-by to Brawley. No excuse. Not even a look at him.

I just walked out.

The noon crowd at the studio looked perfectly normal to me. Ballet costumes, clowns, freaks, the cast of a musical they were shooting. Everybody was normal. The whole world was normal and right. Except me.

She phoned shortly after I returned to the office.

"Jon, I've got to see you right away." Breathless. Desperate.

"Where is he?"

"Out. I don't know ..."

"Okay. The bank. Remember?"

"Yes."

"It's twenty-five after twelve, We'll meet in ten minutes. Can you make it?"

"Yes."

"Inside."

"Yes."

That was all. It was something we had arranged. One of our little secrets. We'd rented a safety deposit box at the Security-First National Bank. It meant plenty of safety to us, even though the box was empty.

I drove over and parked right in front of the drugstore on Burton Way. The sun was shining and the day was warm. But I was cold. It was good to touch the sun-warmed leather of the seat as I got out of the car.

I walked into the bank, not caring if anyone saw me. It didn't matter because I was alone. I went to the rear. Mona was standing there, and it was a shock to see how pale she was, how deep were the rings under her eyes. But she was so neat, so clean, so shining—like the meat of a walnut you've just cracked open.

Without glancing at me, she went through the gate ahead of me. We signed without speaking. When the girl led us inside, I handed over the key.

And then, after years passed, we were alone in the small room, with our empty safety deposit box.

We just moved toward each other. We didn't kiss. We just held on to each other for a long time. Then we stepped apart and sat down on opposite sides of the little table. The electric light was kinder to her, but she looked haggard. She had a stricken look on her face.

"Don't, darling," I said. "It can't be that bad."

Then I saw it. Right near her left temple. A bruise. Right up near the hair line.

"Mona ... where'd you get that mark on your temple?"

"Oh, it's nothing ..."

"Mona, I swear to God, I'll break every bone in his body!" My voice was rising, almost shouting.

You can suffer for someone, and you can feel everything she feels. I found that out. I hurt with every word she said. I hurt for the sense of shame and guilt she felt before him. I winced with her when she had to lie and keep lying. And I gasped with her when he hit her. Because he did. I know he did.

"Please, dear ... Don't. He was drunk. He didn't mean it."

"You're a liar!" I said. "Mona, I'm going over there."

"You're not!" she said. "Don't be a fool. He's much bigger than you are."

Do you realize how deflated I felt? And do you realize how that humiliation enraged me?

"That won't stop me! I'll ..."

"Shut up a moment!" she snapped. "Try to be sensible. I don't want any more trouble, especially with the police ..." She put her hand on mine, holding it tightly. Those long, lovely fingers ... the hand I knew so well, everywhere.

"I don't give a damn about the police. Don't you think I'd kill the bastard if he touched Ann or Sue? Why shouldn't I feel the same way about you? I love you, don't I? Don't I?"

"Yes," she said quietly. "But listen to me. He's wild now ..." She paused. "Jon, he's out on probation and he's bought a gun."

Sure, I'm a hero when it comes to words. But a gun. I'm not a man for guns. Oh, I can handle one. I do better than hit the side of a barn. But that's all. And here was a kid who started with purse snatching and graduated to a gun.

"I'll have him tossed right back into the can," I said.

"That's what I don't want," she said. "Now listen to me."

"What else?"

"He knows I've been seeing somebody, but he doesn't know who you are. At least, he doesn't know yet."

What did that mean? I waited. I was a mummy, wrapped up in cold wet bandages and the wind blew through them to freeze me.

"I don't know why, but I have a feeling Claire Garner knows something. Last night, when she and her husband were over, she kept talking about how much she liked convertible Cadillacs— especially black ones. And she told Bill she always used to walk by here every night when he was in jail. She said she kept an eye on me. And she looked at me very queerly when she said it."

That did it. Guess who had a black convertible Cadillac? Guess who!

"If he finds out," she went on, "I don't know what he'll do. He's half-drunk most of the time, anyway. And he looks ... he looks like a dog that's just been run over." She wasn't looking at me when she said it.

Because I put that look in his eyes. I did it.

She went on. "Sometimes he just lies there, crying ... A big crying lump of ... of ... Bill. What am I going to do with him? If I could get him out of town ... but he won't ... He says he's going to find out who you are. He's that sure ... And if he finds out, he may come to your house ... He may pick a fight with you ... or speak to Sue ... or do anything ..."

A fine sweet mess. Not in the script. Not reasonable. Not neat and planned, the way it had run until now. Not smooth with deceit and cunning. Just plain nasty now.

And suddenly it was *my* danger, not hers. He wasn't threatening her any longer. He was headed for me.

Maybe the Benzedrines began to work now. I don't like to think it was fear pumping my heart so rapidly.

Anyway, it wasn't physical fear. That didn't bother me. But it was the thought that he might get to Sue, might get to the house—yes, and bring it crashing down around my ears. All of it—Ann and home and wife together.

"How could Claire know my name?" I said.

"If she saw the car, she could have taken the license number and got your name that way."

I nodded.

By now I had pulled my hand away from hers. Not that I loved her less, but that all of me was pulling away from her to defend my life with Sue. That desire was so strong that, for the moment, and I know it was only for the moment, the touch of the tigress wouldn't have moved me. I could look at her and still want her. But later ... later ...

"I'll take care of it," I said.

"How? How?"

"I don't know," I said thoughtfully. "But if he does find out ... Well, let me know. Even if you have to phone me at home, let me know."

She nodded. "Darling ... Darling, I wish this hadn't happened ... I wish none of it had happened to us."

"I don't wish that," I said quietly. "I'm glad of every moment of it." I don't know whether that was sincere. Maybe it was, just then. But, by now, I couldn't even trust my own thoughts; I was riddled with lying and deception and cupidity.

But when I said that, she broke.

"Oh, you bastard!" she said softly, with tears streaming down her face. "I love you for saying it—but you shouldn't have. You shouldn't have! How can I have any regrets? How can I keep thinking this is punishment ... and that I deserve it ... and that it wasn't worth it?"

"I can't help it," I muttered.

Then I got up and dried her tears with my handkerchief. I held her close and my chin was on top of her head. She was using Tigress again.

After a while, I opened the door. We almost forgot the safety deposit box.

"I'll think of something," I said as she went out. "Don't worry."

I waited five minutes after she left, then I returned the safety deposit box and went out.

Sure. Don't worry. Let me worry. I've got two halves of a head, because mine's split apart. And two halves are better than one. I'll find the answer. I'll know what to do.

You know what I thought of? You know where my thoughts turned, as they always did when I was in trouble? To Sue. She'd always been there to help. She could listen and understand.

Naturally. Oh, naturally. Walk into your wife's bedroom and ask her please to help you because you were having an affair with another woman, another married woman, and her husband was threatening to make trouble. What shall we do, my dear? Shall we dance?

Hysteria mounts in you like an incoming tide—from your legs to your stomach to your chest and then up into your throat. That's the way it was with me. It was up to my throat. Like a woolen scarf rammed down inside.

CHAPTER 14

I had to run somewhere for help. Wasn't there any place I could find it? Give me a lifeguard station for drowning husbands. Give me a confessional that dispensed freedom from the danger, too. Give me a sign in the sky! Anything!

I couldn't go home. I didn't dare. Sue would see the mark on my forehead. Fear and guilt on my face. Or that widening split in my head.

But maybe I could talk to Kate. She was wise and calm and would know a woman's solution. Or one of the other writers at the studio. Writers knew about these things. Writers planned them on paper and lived through them with their characters. They could write themselves out of trouble.

Well, write me out of this one! Come on, you screwballs and geniuses, write me a fade-out that skirts disaster. Write me a happy ending that preserves my life as it was before. Write this sickness out of my heart.

Sure. It was easy to think that way. But to whom could I speak? There I was in the office—with the telephone before me—and there was nobody to call. A directory full of numbers, a city full of people, a world full of husbands—and nobody to call.

And then my agents walked in, full of energy and self-confidence. My ten-percenters, my two Rocks of Gibraltar, my friends and mentors and business advisers and wet nurses. Script trouble? Hate your boss? Sick of the studio? Want a raise? Unhappy? Call your agents! They'll handle it.

Mine were better than the rest. I could trust them. They didn't horse me around with soft talk and vague promises. They gave it to me straight, always.

But this time I couldn't talk to them. Because they brought more trouble with them.

"We've got a little problem today, kiddie," Stan said. He's the dynamic one—always in there punching, always blunt, always excited, always brimming with an inner pressure he could turn from enthusiasm to rage, like a hose alternating between hot and cold water.

"Oh, I wouldn't say it that way," Garry said soothingly. "Don't make the man think it's that important. It's something we can discuss quietly and maybe get it settled," That was the other partner, slow moving, logical, and the one who always rather apologetically replaced the chips Stan knocked off producers' shoulders.

They made a good team. One banged away without inhibition; the other sighed regretfully and went about mollifying the victim. And the procedure worked. But not on me. Not that time.

"Look, boys," I said. "I've got troubles of my own. Stop gabbing. What goes?"

"Well, Brawley wanted us to talk to you," Stan said.

"Not exactly," Garry said. "He just suggested it. Maybe he thought we ..."

"He's getting pages, isn't he?" I demanded. "He likes what he has, anyway! He said so. What's the matter now?"

"He didn't complain about the script," Stan said hastily.

"What then? The hours I keep? Does he want me coming in like a prep-school kid or stockroom clerk? Nine to six—the way they do at Warner's? If that's the way he feels, tell him to get another boy. I quit!"

"Calm down!" Stan snapped. "What the hell's the matter with you lately? That's why Brawley told us to see you. It's not about the script—it's about you. He's worried about you."

That stopped me. What did he know? I'd been receiving phone calls at the office.... Maybe ... No. It couldn't be that.

"The guy likes you," Garry said. "He thinks maybe you're sick ..."

"Are you?" Stan asked. "You look tired, but a couple of Benzedrines ought to fix you up."

"You want to talk about anything?" Garry said quietly. "If it's money ... or anything we can do ...?"

I was cool and in control of myself. Only I had a cigarette in one hand and my pipe in the other, and I was using them together.

"You can't help me, boys," I said quietly. "Now get the hell out of here."

They looked startled. They knew I couldn't be angry with them for wanting to help me. But Stan looked hurt and indignant,

"See you later," he said, going out. Garry said nothing, but he walked out slowly, watching me until the door closed,

Brawley was my man. Brawley knew what it was to have my kind of home. He had it too—with two children. He'd know. He'd have the answer. He'd help me. I was sure of it.

So I went right down the stairs, and I walked right by Stan and Garry in front of the building. They could have been props, for all the attention they got from me. I was in a hurry.

By now, Brawley was hope and miracles and happy ending. I knew he wouldn't say "excellent" when he heard this situation; but he'd think about it. And I couldn't think anymore.

"The boys told me you were worried about me, so I thought I'd tell you," I said slowly. "Maybe you can see it from another angle. I need help. God, how I need it."

"I'll try to help you, if I can. Go ahead." He picked up the phone and told his secretary not to put any calls through under any circumstances.

He had a large globe in his office, and when I began to talk I whirled it around from time to time, holding my forefinger aimed, toward it. Wherever my finger happened to be when the globe stopped whirling, that's where I wanted to be. The first time, I stopped in mid-Atlantic. That was the place to be. In mid-Atlantic. Drowning. That's where I was, anyway.

I began slowly, omitting a few things here and there because I felt he wouldn't understand them. He was too dignified and circumspect, somehow. But I gave him the story as if it were a script we were doing ... characters, motivations, scenes ... everything ... And while I talked, I felt the jealousy well up inside me. When I told him about Smiley getting out of jail, I could taste a bitterness on my tongue. Maybe that's when I wasn't so careful in expurgating my story. The fear inside me turned to rage, to hatred, to wormwood on the heart. Three months in jail, without his wife ... Three months in jail, thinking about her, wanting her ... Three months' worth of stored up desire ... A punk kid who couldn't ever really know her!

The globe whirled around and, two out of three times, I stopped in mid-Atlantic. Then I hit the Sahara Desert. That was appropriate, too. There was sand in my mouth.

"That's it," I said when I finished. "You see what that no-good bastard can do to me? He can ruin me! He can wreck me from here to breakfast!"

Brawley nodded, but waited for me to stop.

"Isn't there anything I can do? Should I tell my wife before he can get to her? You know how women are. If you tell them about it before someone else does, they feel secure. They can face it down, maybe ... It's the humiliation they fear ... having their friends know about it before they do, feeling people know and are talking."

Now the anger was dying, and the fear came back. I felt removed from everything, hemmed in, with a tall brick wall around me, closing me off from the world. I kept scraping at the mortar between the bricks, scraping at it with my fingernails, wanting to take the wall apart brick by brick. But I couldn't.

"Don't tell her," he said finally. "You can't do that to her ... I couldn't do that to my wife."

That was good to hear. He didn't say he couldn't have done any of the other things to his wife. He didn't say he wouldn't have become involved with Mona.

"Do you see how it happened to me?" I asked pleadingly. "Can you understand how I got into this?"

He nodded. "Look at it this way," he said then. "If you tell your wife, you've anticipated him. But you've done something to your wife that you shouldn't ever do. Things could never be the same between you after that. On the other hand, if you wait—perhaps he won't get to her, after all. Perhaps he'll change his mind. Who knows? And then you'll have done your marriage irreparable damage—and for no reason at all ..."

This time, my finger stopped on nice solid known earth—right in Nebraska. A nice solid place, with fine upstanding citizens. Respectable. Maybe it was an omen.

"I wish I could explain to you how it happened," I said then. "It could have been one of those little slips a man sometimes makes ... An insignificant one ... Lots of men do it ... You know them, too. I know them. And they never get into jams."

"They never meet this kind of woman, either."

"But … I mean, if you could see …"

"Don't explain," he said patiently. "You act as if I'm judging you." He shook his head. "I'll tell you this, even the way you describe it, I might have …" He shrugged. "It's so hard to tell …"

Oh, it was comforting. It was warm and decent. The way he was. But where did it get me? What did it solve?

The globe went around and around again. And there I was right back in mid-Atlantic. Drowning.

So I left Brawley, and I still had to find someone who knew how to deal with this kind of jam. Maybe from another angle. Someone who knew how to deal with sick kids who bought guns … And there was no one but Mac. He could handle it.

And he did.

Mac was a great comfort to me. He knew how to calm me down. His voice was reassuring and his authority unquestionable. This was his terrain—senseless actions, passions, rages, jealousies, and problems connected with firearms. He'd been in them himself, and he'd helped others, too. Privately and professionally. Sitting in his car, I began to regain my sense of values.

First of all, his attitude soothed me. Naturally, under the circumstances, he didn't want any part of Mona now. He was glad he hadn't been caught up in it, and he was self-righteous about it, too. But he'd take care of Smiley for me all right.

"I'll handle it, boy," he said. "I'll just talk to him."

"You talked to him once before. That may have started it all," I reminded him.

"No." He said it flatly. "Right at the start, I told you what his partner said. The guy was always jealous. Without cause."

"That's right." It would have happened anyway. From Mona's story about their marriage, that was a plain fact. I should have known it.

"No, I'll just talk to him," Mac said. "He's on probation. He's got three more months coming if he kicks up any kind of a fuss. All I have to do is warn him."

"I hope you're right."

"You know what happens if we catch him with a gun on him?" he said then. "He's cooked. He's already got a record. And don't forget, Jon, we're not here to protect punks who snatch purses. We're here to protect people like you. Substantial citizens in the community. We know what goes on … We've helped husbands out of jams before. Remember that story I told you about Tripler, the night he had the accident and had that dame in his car?"

That was right, too. Sure. I began to feel like a new man. I was a pillar of the community. Husband and father. Home owner. Possessor of a bank account and a savings account. Man of substance.

"Suppose he comes out to the house—to talk to Sue?"

"He won't. And it won't do him any good anyway. We'll yank him off you and toss him in the can."

"Oh, fine," I said. "That's fine. Get it in the papers."

"I'll handle the papers. Don't worry about that. How many yarns have I told you about picture people? Ever see them in the papers?"

Well, better and better. The sun, which had been out all along, came out a bit stronger. Beating down on me, but friendly now.

"But suppose he tries to get in while the police car isn't around?"

"Don't let him in. If he tries to force his way in, it's illegal entry."

Simple. Smiley was trapped already. If he had any sense, he'd forget about the whole thing. It wouldn't do him any good.

Mac's uniform looked better to me. It had a nice solid look, especially with him in it. Wide black belt. Big pistol. For defending substantial citizens.

It was warm in the police car. The "bennies" make you perspire, too. After all that tension, I was limp and sleepy. But Mac's gun made me think of something else.

"He's got a gun, Mac."

"So what? He's allowed to keep it in his house. Every householder is."

I tried to keep my mind alert, but I was dazed. With fatigue, and, a large residue of undigested fears.

"Suppose he tries to get in? Suppose he just wants to get at me? Suppose he wants to knock me off?"

He looked at me solicitously. "Don't blow your top, boy. It isn't that bad."

"But suppose he does?"

He considered that for a while. "You got a gun in the house?"

"No," I said, surprised.

"You ought to have one. Every householder should. It's protection, even if you never use it."

"What the hell do I want a gun for? This is just a jealous kid trying to make trouble."

Mac shrugged. "He's drunk half the time, isn't he? You ought to be prepared to protect your wife and child." Then he thought for a moment longer, as if making a decision. "Come to think of it, I think I'll tell a couple of the boys up your way to keep an eye on your house. Just cut through your block more often ... Yeah."

"That'll be fine," I said. My castle would be safe. Armed guards outside. A big police car, with two men like Mac in it.

He looked out the window. "A kid like that, once he goes bad ..." He shrugged dubiously. "Like those juveniles ... Hop 'em up with a 'goof ball' and they're dynamite."

I was tired. I was tired. But this kept my attention, fascinating me. I could almost picture it. Smiley, drunk or hopped up, flashing a gun at me, at Ann, at Sue.

"Get a gun," he said finally. "Yeah. You can't tell about a kid like that."

"Mac, you're off your nut. What would I do with a gun? I don't want to kill the guy. I just want him to leave me alone!" I snorted derisively. "You're writing Dick Tracy. What the hell's the matter with you?"

"I'm telling you what to do, boy."

The cars coming from the opposite direction had their windshields in a direct line, and the sun kept flashing into my eyes as they passed. It was continual and hypnotizing. Like the recurrent flash from a lighthouse.

"I've seen cases like this before," Mac said morosely. "Don't think he won't shoot—if he ever comes there with his gun. Crazy kids do, usually. But if you flash a gun at him, he may wilt and beat it. But if he doesn't, kill the son-of-a-bitch. Nobody much will give a damn."

I was appalled. "Mac," I said in horror, "you're out of your mind!"

"Wake up, boy, wake up!" he snapped. "The kid has a gun. He's committing a felony if he tries to break into your house. Armed entry! You're entitled to kill him. He's a purse snatcher—a punk with a record. Why, the boys would cart him off and shake your hand. They don't like kids with guns."

It was cop talk; but it was good talk. I listened, and somewhere on my mind his words engraved themselves, deeper and deeper until they made sense.

"He might come there with that 'unwritten law' crap in his mind," Mac went on. "I don't want you to get hurt. After all, I'm the guy who got you into this. I feel sort of responsible. Fred would be sore as hell at me, too." His usually bland face lit up suddenly. "Hey, another thing. Nobody even knows you know him. If he gets gay with that cannon, he can be lugged out as an unidentified felon ..."

Unidentified felon. Who? Me? I hadn't committed a felony. I'd just broken a Mosaic law, a commandment. What was its number again?

"Okay," I said finally. "But I don't think anything will happen, do you?"

"No," he said. "He'll probably never find out who you are. Even if he does, I think that three months in the can taught him something ..."

"Okay," I said again. "Thanks, Mac. You've saved my life. I was going nuts."

"I know. Sure. Just take it easy, boy. Things will be all right."

We shook hands, and I went off, noticing the sun and the people through a bright glare that was hot behind my eyeballs.

When I reached home, I went into the den and put the gun in a desk drawer. It was just a little one, almost a toy. A thirty-two. Neat and comforting. Meant for pruning big men down to size.

Then I keeled over on the couch and fell asleep. But it was fitful sleep, during which I was conscious of twisting and turning to keep from falling off. Through the wide opening in my split head, centipedes entered, furry and omnivorous, to feed on my brain cells. The tigress stalked in, white and slim and shining, with the gold trapeze-pin stuck into the bare flesh above her breast. And a little man in a beard walked back and forth with a picket sign bearing a large question mark. I screamed at them to help me. The centipedes were devouring my brain. But they didn't hear. And Mac, walking a beat around the rim of my skull, up and down the split edges, never even turned his head to look.

I woke up dry and hot. And the first thing I did was go to the window. Maybe Smiley was outside, hanging around the house, waiting. Every shadow held his menace; every sound was alarming.

But he didn't come.

CHAPTER 15

Thereafter, without admitting that it was too late, I tried to live myself back into my family.

There used to be laughter in my house, but for a long time we'd had very little. It pleased me to think that the house wasn't the same without my presence. But I'd come back now. I wanted in. I wanted refuge. I no longer wanted to be an alien here, looking at Ann from a distance, fenced off from her with my hands stretched through the palings.

Come to Daddy, dear. Come here, Little Doll. Sure I'll play with you, with your dolls and your books and your toys. Why are you looking at me so strangely? Daddy's back. He was away only a short while, writing sonnets to another lady. What's a sonnet, dear? It's a drop of blood squeezed out of your heart—the way it is when you prick your finger with a pin. No, dear; we don't put a bandage on it. It won't help.

With Sue, the process consisted of a resumption of our game playing. Gin and double solitaire and two-handed pinochle. We used to keep score. She was never ahead of me, though I often asked her if she wanted me to let her win a few games. That always got a rise out of her.

It wasn't the games now, it was the attempt to re-establish a pattern of existence. It was the attempt to be a husband again, part of a whole, to fit with her into the complete union of our household.

But I couldn't get back in. For one thing, Sue herself was far away. I felt it, and one night when, we were playing gin, she said so.

"Do you feel there's something wrong between us?" she said abruptly.

At a time like that, it was a fine question. I concentrated on my cards. I read the spots off a Queen of spades. "Why?" I managed to say.

"Well, I feel far away."

"I don't."

"You know what I mean ... It's the kind of thing most pregnant women get. You feel different, and lots of things don't bother you anymore. You're serene and indifferent."

"Maybe that's good."

"But I don't want to feel far away from you."

"Come back," I said. "All is forgiven." My tongue said that; I didn't.

"No, seriously. The doctor said women are more resistant when they're this way ... because of the baby. It gives you a kind of immunity to a lot of illness, too."

Fine. Are you immune to your husband's infidelity, too? Is that part of nature's plan? I wondered whether she heard that come out of my head.

But she went right on, dreamily. "I'll be back soon, Puppy. Don't go away,"

"You won't get rid of me. You'll collect my insurance. The insurance statistics guarantee it. Husbands always die first ... I'll stick around until then." Sure; if a punk with a gun doesn't help the statistical table, I'll be around for a long time.

"Don't talk that way," she said. "You'll outlive me by ten years—you and your hypochondria." She grinned at me and imitated my cocked-head action of taking nose drops. "Any germ you pick up during the day is dead by bedtime. He's sprayed, or drugged, or soaped to death."

"I'm just careful," I said stiffly. Careful; sure. Look at me now.

"I guess I'm a lucky girl," she said smiling. "You don't horrify me when I look at you in the morning—not even with your sleep mask and ear stopples ... you're germ-free ... you're a good provider ... and sometimes you're good for laughs ..."

She leaned over and kissed my hand, and then rubbed her cheek on it.

I couldn't stand it. I couldn't respond. So I just picked a card and went on with the game. It was a good card, too.

"You may be lucky in your choice of a husband," I said, "but don't look now—because I just went gin."

"Oh, you horrible man! I wasn't even looking. I've got forty-four points in my hand!"

No; she wasn't looking. And I was damned glad she wasn't.

Maybe it was fortunate that she felt so far away from me or she might have sensed something wrong.

But she wasn't even close to me, and I couldn't get close to her. I couldn't get back into my home again.

Why didn't it work? Other men slipped from dame to dame in a series of cheap affairs and never stopped. They never got caught. They never suffered remorse or any other penalty. A handful of my friends lived as I had lived before meeting Mona, content with a wife who left no room in heart or mind for anyone else.

Maybe that was the trouble. Maybe that was the trap for men like me. Not the chippies or the shakedown girls. But the rare accidents. There was no involvement with the ordinary casual playmate. But any man might meet someone like Mona ...

The man who did that was sunk. Because you couldn't turn against Mona and toss her aside. You never could want to do that. You couldn't rail against her and despise yourself as thoroughly as you should. You couldn't hate her. Not Mona. Not lovely, wonderful Mona.

You couldn't even hate her now, when every moment was a threat and every ring of the phone a peal of doom. But you could hate her husband.

All along, I clung to the hope that Mac had spoken to Smiley and thrown a scare into him. But that was only because I had to hope or break up. When the weekend went by, I was almost convinced that I was safe. But how could I ever be safe again?

It was Monday night that Mona called. Bill was out with Garner and wouldn't be back for a couple of hours. Could I stop over quickly?

When I arrived, everything she said was a confused jumble of words, not even in her own voice. She was crying hysterically.

"He's raving. He knows about us! I think Claire told him. What have I done to you, darling? He wants to talk to you, and to Sue! He's going to tell her!"

Mac hadn't been able to scare him off. I thought of the police car that had been cruising by more often lately. Mac had told the boys to keep an eye open.

"He won't get to Sue," I said grimly. "I'll kill the son-of-a-bitch!"

"Jon! Don't talk like that! Try to keep your head. Because *I* can't ... Please ..." She couldn't stop the sobbing. "He's just a baby ... crazy jealous ... hurt ... but he can't help it ... I don't want him to be hurt anymore ..."

"Which one of us are you worried about?" I snapped. It was a rotten thing to say.

"You'll be all right ... I know. But don't let him in, please ... Don't talk to him. Make him go away." She sobbed loudly. "Just send him back home."

"Mona."

"I can't stand this, Jon. I can't, I can't, I can't. He's my husband. I've got to stick with him from now on. I've got to think about *him* from now on."

"You don't mean that," I said grimly. "We'll talk about it some other time."

"Forget me, darling, forget me. Please. I can't go on this way!"

"We'll be all right," I said. "I'll take care of him."

Only her crying answered me.

"I love you, Mona ..."

She didn't even answer.

Just the sickening sense of what she'd said remained with me.

Now Smiley was such a threat to me that the mere thought of him made me tremble with rage. He was a threat to my home, to Sue and Ann. I remembered the time I saw that scorpion in the patio, near Ann's sandbox. Its mere proximity to my child sent me into such a fury that I stamped on it, stamped on it, smashing it into the ground with my heel. And long after it was just a wet pulp, I kept grinding my heel down until I was exhausted and limp.

That's the way I felt about Smiley.

That night, for the first time in years, I didn't use my sleep mask or my ear stopples. I wanted to hear every sound, and I wanted to open my eyes and see. Because there wasn't any sleep for me, anyway.

After a while I got up and went down to the den, where I sat in the dark, smoking. I wished I hadn't neglected my friends so much lately. I hadn't seen anyone except the few people we had to dinner. I hadn't even phoned them. Now, it would have been good to talk to someone.

But I just sat there, listening to every sound outside. There's a tree right near the house. Sometimes the wind blows a branch against the roof. It makes a scraping, eerie sound. That night, every time I heard it, even knowing what it was, I jumped in alarm. Later on, I took the gun out of the desk drawer. Just to reassure myself. Because I felt fairly safe. The police car had just gone by again.

You don't know what it is to wait like that, only half living, only half breathing. It gets so quiet you can almost hear the grass growing.

But I knew he'd be there. So I wasn't so surprised when I heard footsteps on the sidewalk. Slow footsteps. Hesitating.

He stood there for a moment. That's when I looked outside. But he was in a deep shadow. I couldn't see him and I couldn't see any signs of the police car. But the way he was standing there made me hope he wasn't too sure of himself or too anxious to tackle a dark house. Maybe he'd come up the steps and ring the bell.

I tiptoed to the basement door, leaned down and yanked the wires to the bell.

Then I went back and waited in the foyer, at the door. The gun was in my pocket, but I wasn't touching it. I didn't even think of it. I was frozen, with my hands at my sides.

Then he started up. I didn't know whether it was just that he was unfamiliar with the steps or whether he was drunk—but he kept stopping. Then he'd come on again.

The light from the street lamp hits a mullioned dormer window beside the door. The crisscrossed pattern was on my feet. The rest of the foyer was dark. His shadow crossed the window. And I waited, and prayed. The bell didn't ring, of course. I never knew whether he pressed it. But then I heard the click of the latch. His hand was on the knob outside. Mine went on to the knob inside.

It was too late now. He just knocked once, when I yanked the door open so it was taut against the guard-chain.

"Get away from here! Beat it!" My voice was low.

"This the Forbes' house?" he demanded loudly.

I couldn't see him. Just the outline of him. The big bulk of him. He was big, all right. He could have taken me apart without getting out of breath. I tried to see him—what he looked like, what his face was like. But he was in the dark with the light behind him.

"Shut up," I hissed. "Everybody's asleep!"

His voice fell. "I want to talk to Forbes ..."

"He's not home," I said. "Now get moving or I'll call the police."

"I'm not afraid of the police," he said sullenly.

But I shut the door. Maybe he'd go. Maybe Sue hadn't heard anything.

Then his voice was loud in the quiet of the night. It must have rung from here to Santa Monica. "I'm not afraid of anybody!" he said.

He still stood there. I listened for a sound from upstairs. I wondered whether Sue had heard. And I waited.

Then he moved, down, away, slowly. He was going! He was leaving. The relief was so sudden that I couldn't move.

And I was still standing there when I heard a sound at the back of the house. He was around in the patio.

My heart stood still for a second, and then began to pump in long loud strokes. What in the hell was he going to do now?

You can't tell about a kid like that. Mac's voice. He'd warned me about this. Sure. And now it was happening. I could hear the creak of the wooden door at the side of the patio.

Inch by inch, I moved to meet him at the French doors that led into the living room. Quietly. My slippers slid along the rug. *Hop 'em up with a goof ball and they're dynamite.*

God, how I wished he'd go away! Quietly, without waking Sue. Or Ann. But he came closer. Bumping into the deck chair outside. It scraped on the flat stone.

Committing a felony. A punk with a record. Anything to stop him. Anything. Please—anything. It's so useless. It won't help anybody. It won't do anybody any good. It'll just wreck me. Just wreck me. Everything I've built up.

I wanted him to disappear in the darkness. I closed my eyes so I wouldn't see anything. But I heard him, closer. *Nobody much will give a damn.*

The Benzedrines were working. My heart was pounding. My forehead was clammy when I put my hand up. Clammy. I was cold. I was hot. I was scared. Mona, keep him away.

Where the hell was that police car? I couldn't even run for them, I couldn't move. I was rooted to the rug, with fear growing out of my pores like branches.

When I heard his hand on the door knob, I opened my eyes. There he was. Outlined ... a big black hulk ... attacking my home ... *Armed entry.* No. Go away. Quietly. The drumming in my head was so loud I couldn't hear him very well anymore. But I had to stop him. *The kid has a gun.* So have I. So have I. Get away from there you ... *Kill the son-of-a-bitch. Kill the son-of-a-bitch. Kill the son-of-a-bitch.*

It went off like a cannon in my hand. Three times. Blasting at him. Wildly.

Then I was standing there, wondering at how the big black shadow was shrinking. It got small. It was melting. It was gone now ...

Was I dreaming?

Oh, no. Because I heard the slam of a car door then. Footsteps up the outside stairs. Sue, calling.

Jon! Jon! What's happened?

Ann began to call. Not crying. Not a bit bothered. "Daddy, I have to go toidy ... Daddy, I have to go toidy ..."

"Sue, for God's sake, tend to Ann!" I screamed.

Somebody was pounding on the door.

"What happened? What happened?" Sue kept saying.

"It's all right. There was somebody trying to break into the house."

I threw the door open. Two cops. I just looked at them dumbly and then down at the gun in my hand. One of them reached over very carefully and took it out of my hand, holding it by the barrel. He wrapped it in a handkerchief. For a minute I leaned against the wall. Then I just sat down, right on the floor in the foyer.

The blackness lasted for a long time. Even after my eyes were open again, nothing registered. Everything was under water, grotesque and slow moving, and voices came to me as through long rubber tubes. Somewhere a siren shrilled. But not here. Somewhere on another planet, maybe. Then lights began to flash under the water and pierce me with brilliant knives.

What had happened to my house? What had happened to my home? Who were these people? They couldn't all be Smiley.

The house was full of people. Two detectives, a fingerprint man, a photographer, and the patrol car men. Every one of them carried a little black notebook; every one of them jotted things down. Outside, the light flashes continued, and a camera was focused on the heap at the living room door.

They kept asking me questions. It was all confused and nightmarish.

"We're just asking," one man said. "After all, no matter who he is, he has a right to his life. Every man has a right to his life." He was pleasant, but firm.

Then some other men came in. One of them took the pressure off me. "Damn it," he said. "I know this guy. His name's Smiley … We had him in for three months. Purse snatching."

They conferred about that. Everybody was much more friendly to me then. Not that they hadn't been before. But they didn't like householders wielding weapons too carelessly. It bothered them. But now they were all for me. It was just a routine matter.

Of course, there were a couple of things. Coroner's inquest. Mortuary. The men who carried the body off.

"How come you guys were here so quickly?" One of the men who came in later was talking to a patrol car cop.

"We had a tip there might be trouble here. Breaking and entering."

Pieces. Fragments. Not in sequence. Somewhere, earlier, there'd been a surprising thing. That was when I said I'd been scared because I could see him holding a gun in his hand.

"What gun?" the detective said, "He wasn't armed."

Half the time I was staring at a little solid glass ornament in the living room. It has colored glass flowers inside of it—bright and cheery, caught forever in glass and never dying.

Somebody went up and spoke to Sue. I did, too. I wasn't up there long, and I don't know what I said. It must have been like a reefer jag, except that I wasn't high. No. I wasn't high at all.

"I thought he was armed," I heard myself saying. "I thought I could see the gun in his hand."

"Yeah, too bad," somebody said. "But don't let it get you, sir. These things happen. He might have had a gun, and he might have killed you ... It's better this way. You are entirely within your rights. We've had too much of this sort of thing around here lately ..."

My rights. Sure. His right was the "unwritten law." Mine was written law. In the code books. Attempted forcible entry. Breaking and entering. Something like that. But he hadn't made it; he never got in.

But the glass was broken in the door. Three small panes. The police figured Smiley had broken the one just over the knob. But I wasn't sure. My shooting was that of a householder, all right. Three shots. One about a foot to the right of him. One in his left thigh. And one, the only one that counted, was right in the head.

Half the time they had to repeat what they were saying. I didn't hear right. My head was still split apart, wide open. A guy who never hurt anyone, a guy who still remembered vividly the emotional upset of stamping on a scorpion—how could a guy like that kill anyone?

You know what kind of a guy I am? I've never hunted because I can't bear to kill anything. I've never fished because I can't bear to put a worm on a hook, much less to rip a fish's jaw apart by catching him. But I killed a man.

"I killed him," I said. "And he didn't have a gun."

But that was all right, though I shouldn't have said it out loud.

The cops were solicitous and a little bit amused. They were used to this kind of thing. They were even used to the horror on the face of the citizen who has his first experience with it.

One detective even got me a glass of water. He assured me everything was all right. "Don't worry about it," he said.

Don't worry. That's what he said. Sue said it, too. She kept reassuring me long after the house was quiet again. In bed with me, comforting me, knowing how horror-stricken I was at what I'd done. But not knowing the reason for my horror.

She tried to give me the same kind of immunity that she had ... a far-awayness, a sense of impregnable security. But it didn't take.

"Darling," she said. "It could have happened to anyone ..." Because all my nasal sprays and vitamins and Benzedrines and salt tablets couldn't kill a centipede in my head.

"You'd feel the same way if a wheel came off the car and you swerved onto the sidewalk," she said. "You might run over someone that way but it would be beyond your control. You'd feel just as awful as you do now ... But it's the same thing, don't you see, darling?"

Oh, yes. I see. I should have waited on Spaulding, and run over Smiley. Hit and run. Not shoot and stay.

"Puppy, darling ... please stop shaking ... and relax ..." she whispered. "Don't think about it. It's a nightmare ... It's ..."

Sure, it's a nightmare. It's an accident. It's everything you want to call it. But it's murder, too. And murder will out, and murder will demand an eye for an eye, and murder will care for its own.

"Why did he have to come here? What did we have that he thought was worth stealing?" she said bitterly.

He was stolen from—not stealing. He came for what was his, though he didn't deserve it. He came for me and for you and for Ann. He came to destroy—and he was destroyed.

But I had a feeling he'd destroy me yet.

Don't worry. Don't worry. Don't worry.

Then it was morning, and the phone began to ring. It kept ringing. Reporters. Newspaper photographers. Gossip columnists. Friends, too. All morning, all day. Checking. Calling for first-hand information. "Why, I heard the whole story ... He told me himself ..." Making jokes about it, too. An interesting tidbit. But trivial.

Don't worry.

But who was worrying?

I was just remembering that Brawley now knew a lot more than anyone ought to know about this. He knew enough to talk to the police. He knew enough to be just as dangerous as Smiley.

But that was ... No. NO!

So I phoned him.

And you know what he said?

"I don't know what you're talking about," he said flatly.

"About the other day ... when I was talking to you ..." I said hopelessly.

"I don't remember a thing about it," he said.

And that was all he'd say.

Call him an accessory. Call him anything you want. But call him a man.

Still, he wasn't the only one who stood in my way now. Oh, no—it went on. There was Claire.

Claire had told Smiley about me. Claire knew the connection between us. Claire was another Smiley—another threat ...

It was a whirlpool. A hurricane. A conflagration. It was me—stunned and disbelieving. Now, I was another Hollywood story, and people would be talking about this in later years. Because I knew it would get out. There was no stopping it.

The night Lupe Velez committed suicide, Mac got the radio call. He went up there and found that an ambulance had already arrived. He walked in, and the phone began to ring. It was a Hollywood columnist, calling to verify the facts. A next-door neighbor, seeing the ambulance in front of the house, picked up the phone and passed the tip on to the columnist. That's how things get out.

This story would leak in another way. The inside story. Whispered. And probably Mac would tell it, confidentially. Another of his yarns.

Another one. That made it easier. Remembering other stories, about other strange people in town. I wasn't alone.

There was the actor who married the most beautiful actress in the picture business—the sexiest, the most desirable, the dream of every red-blooded American—and then blew his brains out because he couldn't satisfy her.

There was a star of the aloof and retiring type, imitating Garbo, who was jaded and cynical and vicious. She'd had her men and her women. Then she moved in on a couple of homosexuals, broke them apart, teased them, tried to make men of them, and finally, knowing all the time what she was doing, waited for them to reach the end of the rope. They did. They sealed the doors and windows and turned the gas on. The papers said it was accidental death due to a faulty gas heater.

I wasn't that bad, was I? Was I?

CHAPTER 16

The inquest took place at a mortuary.

Nothing could have been nicer. They were all prepared for anybody's funeral—at anybody's price. And they could handle me, too.

A coroner's jury of six or seven men assembled to hear the facts. The patrol car cops were there, and I recognized a couple of the other men who had been at my house. A few morticians waited around, and a couple of detectives. And then Mona came in ... with a plain-looking, brown-haired woman accompanying her.

Who could that woman be? What woman did Mona know well enough to bring along with her? Claire ... Only Claire. And what was she doing here? What business had Claire at the inquest?

You know what happens then? You get sick in the stomach and you wait. You hear the words before they're spoken. You hear the accusation. You feel the hand on your shoulder. You die by inches ...

Mona was a widow now, and Mona was free. All the while I waited, I kept repeating that to myself. She looked wan but lovely, her skin whiter than ever, and with a hurt in her eyes. She was broken, but I knew she couldn't hate me. No matter what I did, she couldn't hate me. That's the way it was with us. That's the way it would always be.

She never once glanced my way—which was smart. Here, we were strangers—strangers before the body of her husband. And the sight of him didn't bother me at all.

From the moment I shot him, I'd been like a somnambulist, unfeeling, unseeing, unliving. The impact of that night was like that of the blow that stuns cattle before they're killed. Maybe it was the horror of realizing that I'd shot a man whose face I'd never seen before. I'd shot a man I didn't even know.

And I'd shot him with hatred in my heart.

But Mona wouldn't turn on me. Never. And maybe she'd keep Claire quiet, too.

You'd be surprised how monstrous, how ugly, how horrible

Claire began to look after a while. Every plain feature of her plain face was misshapen into a hideous mask. She could be a Fury, riding me to destruction.

But she didn't testify. She didn't say a word. Why? Because she didn't dare? Or because Mona wouldn't let her? I never knew. But I began to fear that Mona herself might become implicated—as an accomplice, as an accessory.

I didn't know what was going to happen. But you know how it is when you sense something wrong even when everything looks right? That's how it was when the coroner, after whispering with a plain-clothesman, announced that the inquest was postponed at the request of the district attorney.

It came that suddenly.

But why? Why? What was it that sounded like drums in my head? Mona was a widow now, and Mona was free. But why was it that the smell of the mortuary was so strong that I couldn't smell the Tigress perfume as she walked by me. Why was she being cut off from me?

Mona. Claire. Even Brawley. Who had talked?

I watched her as she left. The paleness of her cheek and the black of her hair; the slim animal grace of her; the wonderful leanness of her. And through the open door I saw her get into a police car that was waiting to take her home. Claire got in behind her, and then the driver leaned over to shut the door.

It was Mac.

If ever I loved a man, I loved Mac that day.

Now I knew why Claire hadn't talked. Mac had scared her. Mac had told her that her husband could be sent back to jail to serve the suspended portion of his sentence—another three months— if he became involved with the police. Mac would know how to keep her quiet. He knew about those things.

Maybe … Maybe things would work out …

Oh, I thought that—for an instant. But it was just hoping; not believing.

Because I still didn't know why the inquest had been postponed. Mona hadn't turned on me. Claire hadn't talked. But still there was something wrong. And the more I thought about it, the more I felt I was in a giant trap, and the trap was already closed.

No struggling would help me now—no furious beating against the bars, no tears or anguish or gnashing of teeth.

There was nothing left to do but watch to see who would come to the cage for me, and what he would do with me afterward.

For two days I waited in my cage, docile and puzzled. She didn't phone me, of course. I don't know why I thought she might. Hope, I guess. Despair, too.

The wires had been reconnected to the doorbell, and when it rang that day, it didn't startle me at all. I knew who it was before I opened the door.

It was a couple of men from the district attorney's office. The tall one wondered if I'd mind coming downtown for a conference.

"Just routine," the fat one said. "We've got a car right here. Take you down there and bring you back in no time."

That's what he promised. But I knew better. I didn't care anymore. But I wanted to straighten out one thing. There was still one route open for me, one narrow pathway back into my house. If now, as I had always done before, I could at least be honest, just for this last time, it would bring me close to home again. I wanted that last taste of being a husband and father.

They agreed to wait a while, and I went upstairs and sat down on the edge of Sue's bed. It was a sunny day, and the window was wide open. The tree in front of the house was rich with leaves now. Outside, Ann was pumping furiously at the pedals of her little automobile, shouting gleefully as she swung around into the driveway.

Always before I had been able to tell Sue my innermost thoughts. Until Mona came along. Now, once again, as if reverting to the status of husband under the anesthesia of shock, I could talk. It wasn't just to relieve me. More important than that was my need to re-establish myself with her.

From the beginning, I gave it to her straight. Some little details, the painfully intimate ones, left out to spare her. But I couldn't look at her. My eyes swung around the room, trying to fix on something. The Buddha. No, the lamp. Better the lamp. While I talked, I counted the squares in the thick fabric of the shade. Over and over again.

Not only did I kill Smiley, but in a way I killed Sue. Without looking at her, I knew it. Part of her was gone now and never would come back. Just as I wouldn't. But perhaps it would help her, knowing what had happened to me, knowing how helpless I'd been. That I'd never meant it to happen was no excuse: I wasn't making excuses. I was begging her to understand.

All of it came out—the furtiveness and the hiding, the passion and the confidences, the betrayal and deceit and ignominy. It was my personal Gethsemane.

You want to know what I had? You want to know what it was about my wife that was a thing to be treasured even to the point of killing for it?

Maybe this will tell you.

She cried for me, silently, with the tears coming slowly down her whitened face, and with her blonde hair stirred by the soft breeze that came, through the open window. And this is what she said.

"It's my fault," she said. That's what she said. And she believed it.

Why was it her fault? Because she had been ill and in bed all this time. Because she wasn't well enough to bear a child without taking to her bed for four months or more. Because it wouldn't have happened if we'd gone out together, laughed together, talked more and played more. Because then I wouldn't have been lonely and restless and footloose. It was her fault for withdrawing from me in the aloof and self-contained way of pregnant women. It was her fault because she was obsessed with her weight and her pills and her mineral oil and her diet and her threatened miscarriage. It was her fault because she had failed me. It was her fault.

And she believed it. That's the incredible part of it. She believed it.

And there wasn't anything I could say anymore.

That was our last time in that room together, with the Buddha grinning at me from the bureau and Ann's tiny voice screeching happily outside.

It was almost a masochistic pleasure to go now. Whatever happened, I had it coming to me.

Riding downtown, the two men were more than sociable. They

asked me about my work, how writers found their material, how original stories were bought, how scripts were done. Somehow, I knew I'd never finish that script for Brawley. And then I wondered what would become of the debris in the lower drawer of my desk at the office. Probably the next writer who moved in would just throw all of it into the wastepaper basket. Where I belonged, too.

And downtown, in the district attorney's office, there was a fine large wastepaper basket ready to receive me.

The office was businesslike, and so were all the men in it. The district attorney might have been my father-in-law. He had the same quiet dignity, the same undeviating integrity, the same respect, not for the letter of the law, but for justice and mercy and understanding. But this man behind the desk was a small man with little puffy hands that he held balled-up on the desk top. And he never used an ashtray. He'd stand his cigarette on its end, and all over the desk there were these little white pillars topped off by gray ash.

Still, for all their civility, these men could make their soft voices register inside my head like a calliope with all the stops out. Their voices rattled around the room and bounced off the glass-fronted bookcases.

Right from the first, I kept wishing Mac were there. He knew his way around. He'd know how to guide me. He'd make them go easy with me, too. Maybe I even thought they'd let me walk right out again because I was a friend of his. After all, he'd told me stranger stories than that.

The men in the room began to look like Mac after a while. Fat Mac, thin Mac, red-faced Mac, gum-chewing Mac, and even a Mac with glasses. God, how I wished he'd been there.

"Why did you buy that gun?" the district attorney asked. That was after the preliminaries, after a few smiles and nods and assurances that warmed me up.

I looked at a bookcase. The light on the glass made it act like a mirror, a mirror to my thoughts.

"Well, for … the protection of my household," I said.

"Against whom?"

"Well, maybe it was my imagination. You see, I've got a friend who's a cop ... I mean, an officer. He was always telling me about burglaries and thefts in our neighborhood. Maybe that began to worry me ... I thought the gun was a good idea."

The little balled-up fists didn't move.

"And right after you bought the gun, a burglar tried to get into your house?"

The glass of the bookcase was like a screen. *Smiley was at the door ... her Smiley, Mona's ... the guy who had come back, the guy who had raised his hand to her and bruised that white, white skin. A punk with a record!*

Then another voice broke in. "But he never got into the house."

I didn't react to that. "He broke the glass and was trying to get his hand on the key inside ..."

"No, he didn't." That was gum-chewing Mac, standing near the fat one. "The glass was on the outside. One of your bullets broke it."

The scene changed on the bookcase. *I love yez, Puppy ... in soap on the bath mirror ... we'll have fun together ... blonde hair, not black ... I'll wear clothes that will drive you crazy, and I'll let you rip them off whenever you want to ...*

Red-faced Mac came over and sat on the district attorney's desk. "The people across the way from your house say they heard him at your front door, and he was talking to someone. That was before the shots."

Then the fat Mac scratched the side of his jaw. "That was before they heard the shots."

"Burglars don't come to the front door," the district attorney said softly, standing another cigarette upright on his desk.

Front door? He was at the moat! He was assaulting my home—with words and threats!

"That's ridiculous!" I said.

I could see it in the glass there. *Sue in bed, upstairs. Ann asleep ... He was assaulting them ... my wife and my little girl, whose Daddy had forgotten to fix her blackboard ... and my wife who said it was her fault ...*

"He didn't even have a gun on him," the thin Mac said. "He couldn't have hurt you much—even *if* he'd intended to ... You could hardly say you shot him in self-defense ..."

"But I thought he had a gun. I thought I saw it!"

Self-defense? No. Not defending myself—defending my home, and defending Mona, with a bruise right near that black hairline. *How are you fixed for scruples?*

"You said you'd never seen him before?" the district attorney said.

"I hadn't. I'd never seen him."

"We believe you, sir. But isn't it strange that we found your fingerprints all over his apartment?"

I could see myself there, with Mona, listening to her after she read the sonnet. *It was a dirty trick to give me that ... It sinks us, darling ... Yes, I'm a tigress, and you'd better carry me inside or I'll claw you right here.*

Now all the Macs began hammering away at me, hitting me the way he had hit me that night in front of the bar on La Brea. They hit me with their words. From all sides at once, but leaving no telltale marks. They kept hitting me. And they were beating me to death.

"You know Mrs. Smiley, don't you?"

"We've got proof. Don't deny it."

"Been seeing her regularly for some time?"

"While Smiley was in jail!"

"You're in love with her, aren't you?"

"When he came out, he was in the way!"

"Talk!"

"Isn't that it?"

"So you planned this ..."

"You didn't give him a chance."

"You killed him, and he wasn't even armed!"

"Talk!"

Ann's picture, painted at the nursery school ... a baby fish, a mommy fish and a daddy fish ... Daddy's a fish ... a poor fish ... a sucker ...

"No," I said.

"No," I yelled.

"NO!" I screamed.

But not a sound came out of my throat, and they hammered away at me, quietly, efficiently, the way Mac had done. Only

with words, it was worse. Not a Mac laid a hand on me.
They didn't have to.

You know, for a long time I was sure that Claire had done this
to me. I was sure it was that plain-faced, plain-hearted woman
with envy in her blood.

But it wasn't Claire.

Shortly after I was indicted, when I had my first talk with my
lawyer, it struck me as odd that the district attorney didn't name
Mona in the indictment. She could have been charged with
complicity. Usually, in cases like this, the victim's wife shares the
fate of the other man.

"They have their reasons," my lawyer said. "Maybe she's turning
state's evidence ..." He shrugged. "We'll check on that ... Anyway,
juries don't come tough enough to convict a woman as pretty as
that ... Maybe we can use that ..."

I stepped on that one, hard. If Mona stayed in the clear, it was
all right with me. She hadn't shot Smiley. She hadn't even known
I was going to shoot him. As a matter of fact, *I* hadn't even
known I was going to shoot him. But I figured that I'd pulled that
trigger way back on February sixteenth, when I'd first received
that phone call from Mac.

No. I didn't think it was Mona, either.

Maybe you saw the newspaper photographs of Sue and Ann.
They were taken full face, so Sue wouldn't look so pregnant. I
appreciated that. But no photographer could catch those strange
lights in their blonde hair, or all the wonderful things that shine
from within them.

I had a lovely family, didn't I? Weren't they something to
treasure?

And didn't Sue put up a magnificent fight for me? She called on
everyone for help: on the Screen Writer's Guild; on Brawley; on
Fred Swift; on Stan and Garry, my agents; on all the other
writers I knew, and all the influential people I knew. They wanted
to help me, too. But there wasn't anything they could do.

It wasn't too bad, at first. Because I had the unique privilege of having two women stand up in court for me. That's enough for one man's lifetime. And it was a newspaper sensation, too.

Because the widow of the man I'd killed—a man I'd killed without ever having seen his face—testified in my defense. The widow and my wife stood up together for me. The "other woman" and my wife.

It was good to see, and it was good to know. A man can't ask much more than that, can he?

The courtroom buzzed with it, and everyone took another look at me—to see what kind of a man could still have the victim's wife and his own wife fighting for him. Even the judge took another look at me, and the jury began to pay far more attention to my lawyer.

We began to have a chance.

That was when they brought the record out. Remember that? That's what killed me.

And who brought it out?

Mac!

He said he'd rather cut off his right arm, but he had to perform his duty as an officer of the law. And he looked at me with pity, with his eyes asking forgiveness, and with the great strength of him driving himself up to the witness stand.

The district attorney himself handled the case. It was a big one by then—Hollywood ... picture writer ... names ... the two women testifying in my behalf.

Those little balled up fists were on his hips as he faced Mac.

"You knew the victim during the time he was in the Beverly Hills jail for purse snatching?"

"Yes, sir." Mac's voice was deep and self-possessed.

"You talked with him frequently?"

"Yes, sir."

"And what was your general impression of him?"

"I felt he was going to make trouble for us."

"What kind of trouble?"

The courtroom was still. Sue and Mona were watching me, not Mac.

"I had a feeling he was planning to commit a series of burglaries.

I'd heard him mention something to another prisoner ... but I didn't overhear all he said."

"And what did you do about this?"

"Well, he was due for release ... so I planted a Dictaphone in his apartment on Spaulding. I hoped to obtain evidence that Smiley was going to commit robbery or that he had already committed it."

"And did you obtain this information?"

"No, sir."

Everyone in the courtroom was puzzled. But not the district attorney, and not Mac.

"What did you get?"

Mac looked agonized, as if straining to keep these words from coming out. But they came out. They came out nice and clear and damning.

"A record of a conversation between Mrs. Smiley and the defendant ..."

Then they got out the record and played it for the jury.

That's why Mona wasn't indicted. That's why Mona was in the clear. The only thing that record did was to kill me.

Listen to it. It's a dirge. It's a funeral march. It's death on a record.

"... He knows about us! ... He's going to tell her! ... He won't get to Sue! I'll kill the son-of-a-bitch! ... Jon! Don't talk like that! ... He's just a baby ... crazy jealous ... hurt ... but he can't help it ... I don't want him to be hurt anymore ..."

That brought back the sense of horror ... the appalling terrifying neatness of it. All the cops in the courtroom were Mac. All the cops in the district attorney's office—the cops who kept pounding away at me—were Mac.

I remember now what was in his eyes when he learned I wanted Mona for myself. I remember how he agreed to stay away, but how he questioned me about her, wetting his lips the while. All of it comes back to me with terrible finality. He used a Dictaphone on Fred Swift's wife, too.

The same trick.

But how could I prove it? What did I know that could be shown in court? How could I prove he was the one who had told Smiley about me, stirring him to drunken rages, feeding him the details bit by bit, and holding out my name until the last?

That's what the drumming in my head had wanted to tell me. It was like a tom-tom, telling me not why I was doomed, but just that there was no escape; and the message wasn't signed.

Even now, with the signature plain, I could hardly believe it until it was unmistakable. I didn't believe it. And nobody else would. But I knew. I knew.

The record went on, inexorably. "He's my husband. I've got to stick with him from now on. I've got to think about him from now on ... We'll be all right. I'll take care of him."

It was Mac, all Mac.

He was a good cop. There's no denying that. Everything dovetailed, everything meshed, and Mona was in the clear. It was an impregnable case and nobody but I knew that he had manufactured it.

I was finished. And only I saw the evil behind that bland face, an evil that came out of him like a throttling gas. Like the throttling gas of the execution chamber.

That's when I broke down and began to scream. I remember that. It broke up the session. Because I didn't say a word. I just screamed like a madman.

I knew now that I'd never had a chance since that February sixteenth when I picked up the phone and spoke to him.

Mac was going to get Mona.

THE END

JAY DRATLER BIBLIOGRAPHY
(1910-1968)

Novels

Manhattan Side Street (1936, Longmans, Green)

Ducks in Thunder (1940, Reynal & Hitchcock; reprinted as *All for a Woman,* 1958, Popular Library)

The Pitfall (1947, Thomas Y. Crowell)

The Judas Kiss (1955, Henry Holt)

Doctor Paradise (1957, Popular Library)

Without Mercy (1957, Robert Hale)

Dream of a Woman (1958, Popular Library)

Screenplays
(often with collaborators)

La Conga Nights (1940)

Girls Under 21 (1940)

Confessions of Boston Blackie (1941)

Meet Boston Blackie (1941)

The Wife Takes a Flyer (1942)

Fly-by-Night (1942)

Get Hep to Love (1942)

Laura (1944)

Higher and Higher (1944)

It's in the Bag! (1945)

The Dark Corner (1946)

Call Northside 777 (1948)

That Wonderful Urge (1948)

Dancing in the Dark (1949)

Impact (1949)

The Las Vegas Story (1952)

We're Not Married! (1952)

I Aim at the Stars (1960)

Plays

A Grape for Seeing (1965)

The Women of Troy (1966)

TV Scripts

Robert Montgomery Presents (1950; 1 episode based on *The Pitfall*)

The Revlon Mirror Theater (1953; 1 episode: "Because I Love Him"; teleplay)

The Fabulous Oliver Chantry (1953; creator/writer, TV Movie)

The Desperate Hours (1955; screenplay contributor, uncredited)

Lux Video Theatre (1956; 1 episode: "Impact"; original screenplay)

The 20th Century-Fox Hour (1957; 1 episode: "False Witness"; 1948 screenplay *Call Northside 777*)

Studio 57 (1958; 1 episode: "The Fabulous Oliver Chantry"; creator/writer)

The Thin Man (1958; 1 episode: "A Plague of Pigeons")

Alcoa Theatre (1959; 1 episode: "High Class Type of Mongrel"; story)

Perry Mason (1959; 1 episode: "The Case of the Bedeviled Doctor"; story)

Naked City (1961; 2 episodes: "The Well-Dressed Termite" and "The Deadly Guinea Pig"; writer)

Breaking Point (1963; 1 episode: "Who Is Mimi, What Is She?"; writer)

Burke's Law (1964; 1 episode: "Who Killed Carrie Cornell?"; writer)

The Addams Family (1964; 1 episode: "Lurch Learns to Dance"; story, teleplay)

The New Addams Family (1998; 1 episode: "Lurch Learns to Dance"; story, teleplay)